For a moment Raine closed her eyes, wishing desperately for the chance to go back, to make a better decision.

Caleb's broad hand lightly stroked her back, and she knew his intention was probably to offer comfort but her skin tingled with awareness. She was tempted to reach up to kiss him. Ironically, she was happy to know that she could still feel desire, this deep yearning for physical closeness. That what had happened to her, as awful as it was, hadn't stolen everything.

She still wanted Caleb. The attraction she'd felt for him the moment they'd met was still there.

But would he ever trust her with his whole heart?

Dear Reader

You met Emergency Nurse Raine Hart in THE NURSE'S BROODING BOSS, and I felt compelled to write her story. You may remember Raine as Elana's light-hearted and fun-loving friend—only now circumstances have changed, and unfortunately Raine isn't quite the same person as she was before.

Emergency Physician Caleb Stewart dated Raine for a few months, then they decided to take a break—mostly because Caleb couldn't quite get over his deeply rooted trust issues. Now he wants a second chance, but Raine isn't sure she can lower her defences enough to give him one.

Writing about characters who need to overcome massive hurdles in order to find themselves and to find love is always a challenge. This book was no exception. Raine and Caleb met at the wrong time, but in the end everything happened for a reason and they both grew stronger and closer to each other as a result.

I hope you enjoy Raine and Caleb's story.

Happy reading!

Laura Iding

PS I love to hear from my readers, so drop by my website at www.lauraiding.com and send me a message if you have time.

A KNIGHT
FOR NURSE HART

BY
LAURA IDING

MILLS & BOON

First published in Great Britain 2010
Harlequin Mills & Boon Limited,
Eton House, 18-24 Paradise Road, Richmond, Surrey TW9 1SR

© Laura Iding 2010

ISBN: 978 0 263 21512 0

Harlequin Mi
renewable and
sustainable fo
to the legal en

Printed and b
by CPI Anton

Laura Iding loved reading as a child, and when she ran out of books she readily made up her own, completing a little detective mini-series when she was twelve. But, despite her aspirations for being an author, her parents insisted she look into a 'real' career. So the summer after she turned thirteen she volunteered as a Candy Striper, and fell in love with nursing. Now, after twenty years of experience in trauma/critical care, she's thrilled to combine her career and her hobby into one—writing Medical™ Romances for Mills & Boon. Laura lives in the northern part of the United States, and spends all her spare time with her two teenage kids (help!)—a daughter and a son—and her husband. Enjoy!

Recent titles by the same author:

THE NURSE'S BROODING BOSS
THE SURGEON'S NEW YEAR WEDDING WISH
EXPECTING A CHRISTMAS MIRACLE
MARRYING THE PLAYBOY DOCTOR

This book is dedicated to Senior Editor Sheila Hodgson,
for giving me a chance five years ago
and buying my first book.
Thanks for being so supportive.

CHAPTER ONE

"RAINE! You're here? Working Trauma again?" Sarah greeted her when she walked into the trauma bay fifteen minutes before the regular start of her shift.

Emergency nurse Raine Hart smiled at her co-worker. "Yes, I'm back. Working in the minor care area for a few weeks was a nice reprieve and a lot less stress. But I confess I've missed being a part of the action."

"Well, we sure missed you, too. And I'm so glad you came in early," Sarah said, quickly changing the subject from Raine's four-week hiatus from Trauma to her own personal issues. "I have to leave right away to pick-up my son, he's running a fever at the day care and there's a new trauma coming in." Sarah thrust the trauma pager into her hands as if it were a hot potato. "ETA is less than five minutes."

"No problem." Raine accepted the pager, feeling a tiny thrill of anticipation. She hadn't been lying, she really had missed the excitement of working in the trauma bay. She scrolled through the most recent text message from the paramedic base. Thirty-year-old female with blunt trauma to the head with poor vital signs. Not good. "Sounds like it's been busy."

"Crazy busy," Sarah agreed. "Like I said, we missed you. Sorry I have to run, but I'll see you, tomorrow."

"Bye, Sarah." Raine clipped the pager to the waist-band of her scrubs, and swept a glance over the room. It looked as if Sarah had everything ready to go for the next patient. She was secretly relieved to start off her first trauma shift with a new admission. She'd rather be busy—work was a welcome distraction from her personal problems. Raine was thankful her boss had kept her real reason for being away from Trauma a secret, telling her co-workers only that she'd been off sick, and then reassigned to Minor Care to work in a less stressful environment on doctor's orders. After three weeks in Minor Care, she was more than ready for more intense nursing.

So here she was, back in the trauma bay. Raine took a deep breath and squared her shoulders, determined to keep the past buried deep, where it belonged.

She could do this, no problem.

"No sign of our trauma patient yet?" a low husky, familiar voice asked.

She sucked in a harsh breath and swung around to stare at Dr. Caleb Stewart in shocked surprise. According to the posted schedule, Brock Madison was supposed to be the emergency physician on duty in the trauma bay tonight. Obviously, he and Caleb must have switched shifts.

"Not yet." Her mouth was sandpaper dry and she desperately searched for something to say. Caleb looked great. Better than great. Better than she'd remembered. But she hadn't been prepared to face him. Not yet. She hadn't seen him since they'd decided to take a break from their relationship just over a month ago.

She couldn't ignore a sharp pang of regret. If only she'd tried harder to work things out. But she hadn't.

And now it was too late.

Thankfully, before he could say anything more, the doors of the trauma bay burst open, announcing the arrival of their patient. Instantly, controlled chaos reigned.

"Becca Anderson, thirty years old, vitals dropping, BP 86 over 40, pulse tachy at 128," the paramedic standing at the patient's head announced. "Her GCS was only 5 in the field, so we intubated her. She probably needs fluids but we've been concerned about brain swelling, and didn't want to make her head injury worse."

Raine took her place on the left side of their trauma patient, quickly drawing the initial set of blood samples they'd need in order to care for Becca. Luckily, the rhythm of working in Trauma came back instantly, in spite of her four-week absence. Amy, one of the other nurses, came up on the right side to begin the initial assessment. One of the ED techs cut off the patient's clothes to give them better access to any hidden injuries.

"Raine, as soon as you're finished with those labs, we need to bump up her IV fluids and start a vasopresser, preferably norepinephrine," Caleb ordered. "Shock can kill her as much as a head injury."

"Left pupil is one millimeter larger than the right,"

Amy informed them. "I can't feel a major skull fracture, just some minor abrasions on the back of her scalp. It's possible she has a closed cranial trauma."

Raine's stomach dropped at the news. Patients with closed cranial trauma had the worst prognosis. When the brain swelled there was no place for it to go, often resulting in brain death. And Becca was too young to die.

Suddenly, she was fiercely glad Caleb was the physician on duty. Despite their differences, she knew he'd work harder than anyone to make sure their patient survived. Determined to do her part, Raine took her fistful of blood tubes over to the tube system to send them directly to the laboratory. En route, she noticed two uniformed police officers were standing back, watching the resuscitation. It wasn't unusual to have law enforcement presence with trauma patients, so she ignored them as she rushed back to increase their patient's IV fluids and to start a norepinephrine drip.

"We need a CT scan of her head, stat. Any other signs of internal injuries?" Caleb demanded.

"Bruises on her upper arms," Raine said, frowning at the dark purple spots that seemed to match the size and shape of fingertips. She hung the medication and set the pump to the appropriate rate as she talked. "Give me a minute and we'll roll her over to check her back." She finished the IV set-up and took a moment to double-check she'd done everything correctly.

"I'll help." Caleb stepped next to Raine, adding his strength to pulling the patient up and over onto her side, so Amy could assess the patient's backside. Caleb was close, too close. She bit her lip, forcing herself not to overreact at the unexpected warmth when his arm brushed against hers.

Memories of the wonderful times together crashed through her mind and she firmly shoved them aside. Their relationship was over. She wasn't the same person she'd been back then.

And they had a critically ill patient to care for.

"A few minor abrasions on her upper shoulders, nothing major," Amy announced. Raine and Caleb gently rolled the patient onto her back.

"She's the victim of a domestic dispute," one of the police officers said, stepping forward. "Her husband slammed her head against the concrete driveway, according to witnesses."

Dear God, how awful. A small-town girl at heart, Raine had moved to the big city of Milwaukee just two years ago after finishing college. But she still wasn't used to some of the violent crime victims they inevitably cared for. She tried to wipe the brutal image from her mind.

"Raine?" Caleb's voice pierced her dark thoughts. "Call Radiology and arrange for a CT scan."

She nodded and hurried to the phone. Within minutes, she had Becca packed up and ready to go.

"I'm coming with you," Caleb said, as she started pushing the cart towards the radiology suite next door. Thankfully the hospital had had the foresight to put the new radiology department right next to the emergency department. "I don't like the way her heart rate is continuing to climb. Could be partially due to the norepinephrine, but it could also be her head injury getting worse."

She couldn't argue because Becca's vital signs were

not very stable. Usually the physicians only came along on what the nurses referred to as road trips, for the worst-case scenarios.

As Becca's blood pressure dropped even further, Raine grimly acknowledged this was one of those times she would be glad to have physician support.

She was all too aware of Caleb's presence as they wheeled the patient's gurney into the radiology suite. There were unspoken questions in his eyes when he glanced at her, but he didn't voice them. She understood—this was hardly the time or the place for them to talk about the mistakes they'd made in the past. About what might have been.

She kept her gaze focused on their patient and the heart monitor placed at the foot of her bed. They were only part way into the scan when Becca's blood pressure dropped to practically nothing.

"Get her out of there," Caleb demanded. The radiology tech hurried to shut down the scanner so they could pull the patient out from the scanner opening. "Crank up her norepinephrine drip."

Raine was already pushing buttons on the IV pump. But then the pump began to alarm. She looked at the swollen area above the patient's antecubital peripheral IV. "I think her IV is infiltrated."

Caleb muttered a curse under his breath and grabbed a central line insertion set off the top of the crash cart the radiology tech had wisely brought in. "Then we'll put a new central line in her right now."

"Here?" the radiology tech asked incredulously.

Caleb ignored him. Raine understood—they couldn't

afford to lose another vein. A central line would be safer in the long run. Anticipating his needs, she quickly placed sterile drapes around the patient's neck, preparing the insertion site as Caleb donned sterile gloves. Luck or possibly divine intervention was on his side when he hit the subclavian vein on the first try.

"Here's the medication," Raine said, handing over the end of the IV tubing she'd disconnected from the non-working IV.

The moment Caleb connected the tubing, she administered a small bolus to get the medication into her patient's bloodstream quicker, since the woman's blood pressure was still non-existent and her heart rate was dropping too. For a moment, Raine held her breath, but their patient responded well and her blood pressure soon returning to the 80s systolic. Caleb anchored the line with a suture and then quickly dressed the site.

But they weren't out of the woods yet. Worried, she glanced at Caleb. "Should we complete the scan?" she asked.

He gave a curt nod, his expression grave. One of the things she liked best about Caleb was that he didn't build a wall around himself to protect his emotions. He sincerely cared about his patients. "We have to. The neurosurgeons are going to need to see the films in order to decide whether or not to take her to surgery."

The radiology tech didn't look very happy at the prospect, but took his place to continue running the scan. Raine and Caleb together slid the patient back onto the exam table. She was startled when he took her arm, and instinctively pulled away. She winced when she realized what she'd done, knowing he'd done nothing to deserve her reaction. Her issues, not his.

His stormy gray eyes darkened with hurt confusion but she avoided the questioning look he shot her way. She felt bad about hurting him again, but at that moment her patient's heart monitor alarmed so she was forced to go over to adjust the alarm limits. The ten-minute exam seemed excruciatingly long, but they finally finished the procedure.

Caleb didn't say anything as they pushed the gurney back to the trauma bay. The moment they arrived, he crossed over to page the neurosurgeon to discuss the best course of action for their patient.

"Becca?" Raine glanced over at the shrill voice. She saw Amy bringing in a woman who looked to be a few years younger than their patient. "Oh, my God, Becca. What did he do to you?"

Raine had to turn away from the crying woman who clutched their patient's hand.

"Her sister, Mari," Amy said in a low tone. "I had to let her in because I'm betting Becca will be going to the OR ASAP."

"Of course you did," Raine said, but her voice sounded far away, as if she was speaking through a long tunnel. She'd wanted to be busy, but maybe she'd been overconfident. Maybe she wasn't ready for the trauma room just yet. Maybe she should have stayed longer in the minor care area of the ED, where they didn't deal with anything remotely serious.

Her eyes burned and she fought the need to cry right along with Mari. She turned away, to give them some privacy and to pull herself together. She went over to the computer to look up Becca's most recent labs.

"Raine? Are you all right?" Caleb asked, coming up to the computer workstation.

"Of course." She subtly loosened her grip on the edge of the desk and forced herself to meet his gaze, hoping he couldn't tell how emotionally fragile she was. It was far too tempting to lean on Caleb's strength. To confide in him. If things had been different…

But they weren't. Reminding herself that she needed to find her own strength to work through her past, she waved a hand at the computer screen. "Did you see these latest results? Her electrolytes are way out of whack."

He gave her an odd look, but then nodded. "Get her prepped for the OR. Dr. Lambert wants her up there ASAP."

"Okay." Raine abandoned her computer and jumped to her feet. She hurried over to Becca's bedside and told Amy and Mari the news.

Within moments she and Amy transported Becca up to the OR, releasing her into the hands of the neurosurgeons. There was nothing else they could do for now but wait.

Raine tried to push Becca's fate out of her mind since she and Caleb had done everything she could for the patient. But concentrating on her job wasn't easy. Especially when she could feel Caleb's gaze following her as she worked.

She could tell he wanted to talk. The very thought filled her with dread. She couldn't talk to him now, no matter how much she wished she could.

It was too late. She'd missed her chance to take his

calls weeks ago. Better now to focus her energy on moving forward rather than rehashing the past.

What she and Caleb had once shared was over.

"Dr. Stewart?" He glanced up when Raine called his name. "I think you'd better check Mrs. Ambruster's chest X-ray. Her breathing has gotten dramatically worse."

Caleb scowled at the formal way she addressed him. They'd dated for almost two months, had shared more than one passionate kiss. He knew it was his fault that she'd requested a break from their relationship but, still, hadn't they moved well beyond the *Dr. Stewart* stage?

"Sure." A surge of regret washed over him. Seeing Raine again made him realize he'd never gotten over her. Not completely. If only he'd handled things differently. If only he hadn't been such an ass.

He'd heard she'd moved over to the minor care area because she'd needed a break from Trauma. He knew full well she'd really needed a break from him.

And he'd missed working with her, more than he'd wanted to acknowledge.

He gave himself a mental shake. This wasn't the time or the place. He crossed over to the patient, who had come in with vague flu-like symptoms that he was beginning to suspect was something much more complicated. Using the closest computer terminal, he pulled up the patient's chest X-ray. Raine was right, the patient's breathing must be severely compromised as the X-ray looked far worse. He suspected the large shadow was a tumor and likely the cause of a massive infiltrate on the right side of her lungs, but she would need more of a work-up to be sure. "How much O2 do you have her on?"

"Six liters."

He frowned. "Crank her up to ten liters per minute and prepare for a thoracentisis."

Raine did as he asked, although he noticed she gave him a wide berth whenever he came too close.

He was troubled by the way Raine was acting. He regretted the way he'd overreacted that night and had tried to call her several times to apologize but she hadn't returned his calls. Did she still blame him? Was it impossible for her to forgive him?

Seeing her tonight brought his old feelings back to the surface. Along with the same sexual awareness that had shimmered between them from the very first time they'd met.

But as much as that sensation was still there, something was off. He'd noticed right from the start of their shift how her usual enthusiasm was missing. Maybe it was just the seriousness of their domestic violence patient, but they'd shared tough shifts before. Somehow this was different, especially the way she seemed to avoid him whenever he came too close.

Maybe she was worried he'd ask her out again. And he had to admit, the thought had crossed his mind. More than once. Sure, he'd made a stupid mistake before, but didn't he deserve a second chance?

Apparently, Raine wasn't willing to grant him one.

He turned to their elderly patient, focusing on the procedure he needed to do. He put on a face mask and then donned sterile gown and gloves, while Raine prepped the patient. He lifted the needle and syringe in his hand and gently probed the space between the fourth and fifth ribs. He numbed the area with lidocaine and then picked up the longer needle used to aspirate the fluid. Slowly, he advanced the needle.

He hit the pocket of fluid and held the needle steady while the site drained. Once he'd taken off almost a liter of fluid, their patient's oxygen saturation improved dramatically.

"Place a dressing over this site, would you?" he asked Raine. "And we need to send a sample of this fluid to Pathology." Stepping back, he stripped off his sterile garb. Once she'd gotten the specimens sent to the lab and the patient cleaned up, he went back in to talk to the husband and wife.

"Mrs. Ambruster, I'm afraid your chest X-ray shows something abnormal and I believe whatever is going on is causing fluid to build up in your lungs."

The elderly couple exchanged a look of dismay. "What is it? Cancer?" her husband asked.

Caleb didn't want to lie but at the same time he didn't honestly know for certain what the problem was. He was impressed by the mutual love and respect this elderly couple displayed toward each other, something missing from his own family life. He tried to sound positive. "That is one possibility but there are others that could be less serious. I'm not a thoracic surgeon, but I'd like to refer you to one. I can arrange for you to see someone first thing in the morning if you're willing."

The Ambrusters agreed and he made the arrangements with the thoracic surgery resident. By the time he wrote the discharge orders for Mrs. Ambruster, the oncoming shift had arrived.

He was free to go home. But he didn't want to leave, not without talking to Raine.

He found her in the staff lounge, but stopped short when he realized she was crying. Immediately concerned, he rushed over. "Raine? What's wrong?"

"Nothing." She quickly swiped at her eyes, as if embarrassed by her display of emotion.

"Raine, please. Talk to me." He couldn't hide the desperate urgency in his voice.

There was a slight pause, and he found himself holding his breath when she finally brought her tortured gaze up to meet his. "Becca died. She never made it out of surgery."

Caleb grimaced beneath a wave of guilt. Here he'd been worried about himself when Raine was grieving over their patient. "I'm sorry, Raine. I didn't know."

"Doesn't matter. We did what we could."

The despair in her tone tugged at his heart. He wanted to reach out to her, but knew he'd given up that privilege when he'd accused her of cheating on him.

He wanted to apologize. To explain he now knew he'd been wrong, but where to start?

"I have to go," Raine muttered, swiping at her face and attempting to brush past him.

"Wait." He reached out to grasp her arm. "Please don't go. Let's talk. About us. About where we went wrong."

"There's no point. What we had is over," she whispered, wrenching from his grasp. The hint of dark desperation shadowing her eyes hit hard. She hesitated only for a moment, before ducking out of the room.

Shocked, he could only stare after her. Something was definitely wrong. This wasn't just Raine wanting to take a break from their relationship. There was something more going on.

He'd screwed up before, but he wouldn't give in so easily this time. He was determined to uncover the truth.

CHAPTER TWO

RAINE drove home, wishing she hadn't lost control like that in front of Caleb. It was her own fault that he had no idea what she'd been through. No one did. She been too embarrassed, too ashamed. Feeling too guilty to tell anyone.

She was determined to get over the past, and she knew that moving forward was the best way to accomplish that. And if she regretted taking a break from her relationship with Caleb, she had no one to blame but herself.

Caleb had trust issues. But instead of trying to work through them, she'd broken things off. And then, when he'd tried to call to make up, she hadn't returned his calls.

Because by then everything had changed.

She'd thought she'd put the past behind her. But obviously she'd jumped back into the trauma environment a little too quickly. She'd taken off work completely for a week, and then had taken a three-week assignment in the minor care area, trying to ease herself back into the stressful working environment the way her counselor had suggested. Obviously, she had a way to go before she'd be back to her old self.

She pulled into her assigned parking space in the

small lot behind her apartment, threw the gearshift into park and dropped her forehead on the steering-wheel with a deep, heavy sigh.

Who was she trying to kid? She'd never be the person she had been before. Hadn't her counselor drilled that fact into her head? There was no going back. The only option was to move forward.

Firming her resolve, she climbed from the car and headed up to her second-story apartment. She smiled when her cat, Spice, meowed softly and came running over to greet her, rubbing up against her leg with a satisfied purr. She picked up the cat and buried her face in the soft fur. She'd adopted Spice from the local shelter a few weeks ago and had not regretted it. Coming home to an empty apartment night after night had been difficult. Spice made coming home much easier. And the cat gave her someone to talk to.

She threw a small beanbag ball past Spice—the goofy cat actually liked to play fetch like a dog—and tried to unwind from the long shift. But the relaxation tips her therapist had suggested didn't help and she still had trouble falling asleep. She'd taken to sleeping on her sofa, and as she stared at the ceiling, she thought about her counselor's advice to confide in someone. She knew her counselor might be right, but she just couldn't make herself take that step.

If she told one of her friends what had happened, they'd look at her differently. With horror. With pity. Asking questions. She shivered with dread. No, she couldn't stand the thought of anyone knowing the gory details. Especially when she couldn't remember much herself.

The one person she might have confided in was Caleb. If he'd trusted her. Which he didn't.

The events of that night when he'd looked at her with frank disgust still had the power to hurt her. She'd gone out to a local pub with a group of ED staff nurses and physicians after work. Jake, one of the new ED residents, had flirted with her. She hadn't really thought too much about it until the moment she'd realized he'd had too much to drink. He'd leaned in close, with his arm around the back of her chair, trying to kiss her.

Before she could gently, but firmly push him away, Caleb had walked in. She'd blushed because she knew the situation looked bad, but he hadn't given her a chance to explain. Instead, he'd accused her of seeing Jake behind his back.

She'd seen the flash of hurt in his eyes, but at the same time she hadn't appreciated Caleb's willingness to think the worst of her. She'd talked to him the next day, and had tried to explain. But when he'd sounded distant, and remote, she'd given up, telling him it might be best to take a break from their relationship for a while.

She'd been stunned when he'd agreed.

Pounding a fist into her pillow, she turned on the sofa and tried to forget about Caleb. With everything that had happened, she'd put distance between herself and her friends.

Her closest friend, Elana Schultz, had recently married ED physician Brock Madison. In the months since their wedding she hadn't seen as much of Elana. They were still friends, but Elana had a new life now with Brock.

When Elana had assumed Raine had taken the job in Minor Care to avoid Caleb, she hadn't told her friend any different.

It was better than Elana knowing the truth.

The next morning Raine's phone woke her from a deep sleep. She patted the mound of linens on her sofa, searching for her cellphone. "Hello?"

"Raine? It's Elana. I just had to call to tell you the news."

"News?" Elana's dramatically excited tone brought a smile to her face. She pushed a hand through her hair and blinked the sleep from her eyes. "What news?"

"We heard the baby's heart beat!" Elana exclaimed, her excitement contagious. "You should have seen the look on Brock's face, he was so enthralled. He brought tears to my eyes. You'd never guess he once decided to live his life without children."

"He was delusional, obviously," Raine said dismissively. "And that was long before he met you. I'm so excited for you, Elana. Did you and Brock change your mind about finding out the baby's gender?"

"No, we still want the baby's sex to be a surprise. But my due date is confirmed—five months and one week to go."

Raine mentally calculated. It was the seventh of June. "November fifteenth?"

"Yes, give or take a week. Brock is painting the baby's room like a madman—he's worried we won't have everything ready in time," Elana said with a laugh. "I keep telling him there's no rush."

"Knowing Brock, he'll have it ready in plenty of

time." Raine tried to hide the wistful tone of her voice. Watching Elana and Brock together was wonderful and yet painful at the same time. They were so in love, they glowed.

If only she were worthy of that kind of love. She pushed aside the flash of self-pity. "Do you have time to meet for lunch?" she asked.

"Oh, I'm sorry Raine. I'd love to, but I agreed to volunteer at the New Beginnings clinic this afternoon. Can I take a rain-check?"

"Sure." Raine forced lightness into her tone. The New Beginnings clinic was a place where low-income patients could be seen at no cost to them. She'd volunteered there in the past, but not recently. "No problem. Take care and I'm sure I'll see you at work one of these days."

"I know, it's been for ever, hasn't it?" Elana asked. Raine knew it was exactly one month and three days since they'd worked together. Since her life had irrevocably changed. "You've been working in the minor care area and I've been cutting back my hours now that I'm pregnant. The morning sickness has been awful. Brock is being a tad overly protective lately, but I'm not going to complain. I'm scheduled to work this weekend."

"Great. I'm working the weekend, too and I'm back on the schedule in the trauma bay. I'll see you then." Raine hung up the phone, feeling a bit deflated. Not that she begrudged her friend one ounce of happiness. Elana had gone through some rough times, too.

Elana had moved on from her painful past, and Raine was sure she could too. One day at a time.

Since the last thing she needed was more time on her

hands, Raine forced herself to climb out of bed. There was no point in wallowing in self-pity for the rest of the day.

She needed to take action. To focus on the positive. She'd taken to volunteering at the animal shelter on her days off, as dealing with animals was somehow easier lately, than dealing with people.

It was time to visit her furry friends who were always there when she needed them.

Caleb pulled up in front of his father's house and swallowed a deep sigh. His father had called to ask for help, after injuring his ankle after falling off a ladder. His father was currently living alone, as his most recent relationship had ended in an unsurprising break-up. Caleb was relieved that at least this time his father had been smart enough to avoid marrying the woman. With four divorces under his belt, you'd think his father would learn. But, no, he kept making the same mistakes over and over again.

Leaving Caleb to pick up the pieces.

He walked up to the house, frowning a bit when he saw the front door was open. He knocked on the screen door, before opening it. "Dad? Are you in there?"

"Over here, Caleb," his father called out. His father's black Lab, Grizzly, let out a warning bark, but then came rushing over to greet him as he walked through the living room into the kitchen. He took a moment to pet the excited dog, and then crossed over to where his father was seated at the table, with his ankle propped on the chair beside him. "Thanks for coming."

"Sure." He bent over his father's ankle, assessing the

swollen joint, tenderly palpating the bruised tissue around the bone. "Are you sure this isn't broken?"

"Told you I took X-rays at the shelter, didn't I?" his father said in a cantankerous tone. "It's not broken, it's only sprained. Did you bring the crutches?"

"Yes, they're in the car." But he purposely hadn't brought them in. He'd asked his father to come into the ED while he was working, but did he listen? No. His father had taken his own X-rays on the machine he used for animals. Caleb would rather have looked at the films himself.

"Why did ya leave them out there? Go get 'em."

Caleb propped his hands on his hips and scowled at his father. "Dad, be reasonable. Take a couple of days off. Being on crutches around animals is just asking for trouble. Surely the shelter can do without you for a few days?"

"I told you, there's some sort of infection plaguing several of the new animals. I retired from my full-time veterinary practice last year, didn't I? I only go to the shelter three days a week and every other Saturday. Surely that's not too much for an old codger like me." His dad yanked on the fabric of his pants leg to help lift his injured foot down on the floor. "If you won't drive me, I'll arrange for a cab."

Caleb closed his eyes and counted to ten, searching for patience. He didn't remember ever calling his dad an old codger, but nevertheless a shaft of guilt stabbed deep. He'd promised to help out more, but hadn't made the time to come over as often as he should have. "I said I'd take you and I will. But, Dad, you have to try taking it easy for a while. Every time I stop by I find you doing something new. Trying to clean out the gutters on that rickety old ladder was what caused your fall in the first place."

"Well, someone had to do it."

This time Caleb counted to twenty. "You never asked me to help you with the gutters," he reminded his father, striving for a calm tone. "And if you'd have waited, I could have done the job when I came over to mow your lawn on the weekend."

His father ignored him, gingerly rising to his feet, leaning heavily on the back of the kitchen chair to keep the pressure off his sore ankle. Grizzly came over to stand beside him, as if he could somehow assist. "I'm going to need those crutches to get outside."

Arguing with his father was about as effective as herding cats. His father simply ignored the things he didn't want to deal with. "Sit down. I'll get them." Caleb strode back through the house, muttering under his breath, "Stubborn man."

He grabbed the crutches out of the back of the car and slammed the door with more force than was necessary. He and his father had always been at odds and the passing of the years hadn't changed their relationship much. Caleb's mother had taken off, abandoning him at the tender age of five. One would think that fact alone would have brought him and his dad closer together. But his father hadn't waited very long before bringing home future stepmothers in an attempt to replace his first wife. At first the relationships had been short-lived, but then he'd ended up marrying a few.

None of them stayed very long, of course. They left,

just like his mother, for a variety of reasons. Because they realized being a vet didn't bring in a boat-load of money, especially when you were already paying alimony for a previous marriage. Or they found someone else. Or simply got bored with playing step-mom to someone else's kid.

Whatever the reason, the women his father picked didn't stick around. Carmen was the one who'd stayed the longest, almost three years, but in the end she'd left, too.

Yeah, his father could really pick them.

"Here are the crutches," he said as he entered the kitchen. "Now, be patient for a minute so I can measure them. They have to fit your frame."

For once his father listened. After he'd adjusted the crutches to his father's height, the older man took them and leaned on them gratefully. "Thanks," he said gruffly.

"You're welcome." Caleb watched his father walk slowly across the room, making sure he could safely use them. Grizz got in the way once, but then quickly learned to avoid them. Crutches weren't as easy to use as people thought, and Caleb worried about his father's upper-arm strength. But his father was still in decent shape, and seemed to manage them well enough. Reluctantly satisfied, he followed his father outside, giving Grizz one last pat on the head.

The shelter was only ten miles away. Neither one of them was inclined to break the silence as Caleb navi-gated the city streets.

He pulled up in front of the building and shut the car. "I'll come inside with you," he offered.

"Sure." His father's mood had brightened the closer

they'd gotten to the shelter, and Caleb quickly figured out the elder man needed this volunteer work more than he'd realized.

More guilt, he thought with a slight grimace. He held the front door of the building open, waiting for his father to cross the threshold on his crutches before following him in.

"Dr. Frank! What happened?"

Caleb froze when he saw Raine rushing toward his father. She didn't seem to have noticed him as she placed an arm around his father's thin shoulders.

"Twisted my ankle, that's all. Nothing serious." His father patted her hand reassuringly. "Now, tell me, Raine, how's Rusty doing today? Is he any better?"

"He seems a little better, but really, Dr. Frank, should you be here? Maybe you should have stayed at home to rest." Raine lifted her gaze and he knew she'd spotted him when she paled, her dark red hair a stark contrast to her alabaster skin. "Caleb. What are you doing here?"

"Dropping off my father." He couldn't help the flash of resentment at how friendly his father and Raine seemed to be. She had never mentioned working at the animal shelter during those two months they'd dated. But here she was, standing with her arm protectively around his father, as if they were life-long buddies.

A foreign emotion twisted in his gut. Jealousy. For a moment he didn't want to acknowledge it. But as he absorbed the camaraderie between his father and Raine, he couldn't deny the truth.

His father had grown closer to Raine in the time since she'd pushed him away.

* * *

Raine couldn't believe that Dr. Frank was actually Caleb's father. She'd never really known if Frank was the retired vet's first or last name, and hadn't asked. They'd had an unspoken agreement not to pry into each other's personal lives. But now that she saw the two of them in the same room, the resemblance was obvious. Dr. Frank's hair was mostly gray, whereas Caleb's was dark brown, but the two men shared the same stormy gray eyes and aristocratic nose. Of course, Caleb was taller and broader across the shoulders but his dad was no slouch. In fact, she thought Dr. Frank was rather handsome, all things considered.

Caleb would age well, if his father's looks were any indication. And for a moment regret stabbed deep. As much as she needed to move forward, it was difficult not to mourn what might have been.

"What time do you want me to pick you up?" Caleb asked his father.

"I can give Dr. Frank a ride home if he needs one," she quickly offered.

Caleb's eyebrows rose in surprise, as if he suspected she had some sort of ulterior motive. Was he assuming she was trying to get back into his good graces by helping his father? If things were different, she might have been tempted.

"That's very kind of you, Raine," Dr. Frank said. She could have sworn the older man's gaze was relieved when he turned back toward his son. "There's no need for you to come all the way back out here, Raine will drive me home. Thanks for the ride, Caleb. I'll see you this weekend, all right?"

"Yeah. Sure." For a moment Caleb stared at her, as

if he wanted to say something more, but after a tense moment he turned away. She had to bite her lip to stop herself from calling out to him as he headed for the door. "See you later, Dad," he tossed over his shoulder.

He didn't acknowledge Raine as he left. And even though she knew it was her fault, since taking a break from their relationship had been her idea, she was ridiculously hurt by the snub.

Trying to shake off the effects of her less than positive interaction with Caleb, she faced Dr. Frank. "So, are you ready to get to work?"

Caleb's father's glance was sharp—she should have known he wouldn't miss a thing. "Do you and my son know each other?"

She tried to smile. So much for their rule to stay away from personal things. "Yes, we both work in the emergency department at Trinity Medical Center," she admitted. "Caleb is a great doctor, everyone enjoys working with him."

"Everyone except you?"

She flushed, hating to think she'd been that transparent. Especially when she liked working with Caleb. Too much for her own good. "I like working with him, but I'm thinking of changing my career to veterinary medicine," she joked, in an attempt to lighten things up. "Maybe you'll give me some tips, hmm? Come on, let's head to the back. I think I should take a look at that ankle of yours."

"Caleb already looked at it." Dr. Frank waved her off. "I'm more interested in the animals. I'm going to need you to bring them to me in the exam room as my mobility is limited."

"No problem." Raine wanted to help, but as he deftly maneuvered the crutches, she realized he was doing fine on his own.

Dozens of questions filtered through her mind, but she didn't immediately voice them. Caleb obviously hadn't mentioned her to his father during the time they'd been seeing each other, which bothered her. Especially since he hadn't even talked about his father very much.

What else didn't she know about him? And why did it matter? What she and Caleb had was over. For good. No matter how much she missed him.

Dr. Frank didn't notice her preoccupation with his son. His attention was quickly focused on the sick animals.

She brought Rusty into the room, the Irish setter puppy they'd rescued three weeks ago. She'd fallen for Rusty in a big way, especially when everyone teased her that Rusty's dark red coat was the same color as her hair. But unfortunately the lease on her apartment didn't allow dogs, which was why she'd taken Spice, the calico cat, instead.

But when she did have enough money saved to buy a house, she planned on adopting a dog, too. Hopefully one just as sweet tempered and beautiful as Rusty.

"There, now, let me take a listen to your heart," Dr. Frank murmured as he stroked Rusty's fur. The dog had been in bad shape when he'd been picked up as a stray, and he'd shied away, growling at men, which made them think he might have been abused. Raine didn't know how long he'd been on the streets, but he'd been dangerously malnourished when he'd arrived. And he'd been sick with some sort of infection that had soon spread to the animals housed in the kennels near him.

She held the dog close, smiling a little when he licked her arm. "You're such a good puppy, aren't you?"

"He's definitely doing better on the antiviral meds we've been giving him," Dr. Frank announced, finishing his exam. "Let's move on to Annie, the golden retriever."

Volunteering at the shelter had saved her from losing her mind in her dark memories. Raine found she loved working with the animals. The hours she spent at the shelter flew by. She barely had enough time to run home to change, after dropping off Dr. Frank, before heading off to work.

As she entered the emergency department, she saw Caleb standing in the arena. When his gaze locked on hers, her stomach knotted with tension. Was she really up for this? Working in Trauma with Caleb? She quickly glanced around, looking for the charge nurse, determined to avoid being assigned to his team.

Unfortunately, there were only two trauma-trained nurses on duty for the second shift, so she had no choice but to work in the trauma bay. And, of course, Caleb was assigned to the trauma bay as well.

Her stomach continued to churn as she took report from the offgoing nurse. As they finished, a wave of nausea hit hard, and she put a hand over her stomach, gauging the distance to the bathroom.

She swallowed hard, trying to figure out what was wrong. Could she have somehow gotten the virus that seemed to be plaguing the animals at the shelter? She'd have to remember to ask Dr. Frank if animal-to-people transfer was even possible.

Sipping white soda from the nearby vending machine helped and Raine tried to concentrate on her work. They'd transferred their recent patient up to the ICU but within moments they'd received word that Lifeline, the air-rescue helicopter, had been called to the scene of a crash involving car versus train.

Sarah, the other trauma nurse on duty, was restocking the supplies so Raine used the few moments of free time to head into the bathroom.

As she fought another wave of nausea, she leaned over the sink and thought of Elana. This must be how her friend had felt with her horrible bouts of morning sickness.

Her eyes flew open at the implication and she stared at her pale reflection in shock. Could it be? No. Oh, no. She couldn't handle this.

Her knees went weak and she sank down onto the seat of the commode. Counting backwards, the sickness in her stomach threatened to erupt as she realized it had been just over four weeks since her last period.

CHAPTER THREE

DEAR God, what if she was pregnant?

No, she couldn't be. There was just no way she could handle this right now. Especially considering the circumstances under which she might have conceived. She shied away from the dark memories.

She didn't have time to fall apart. Not when there was a serious trauma on the way. Car versus train, and the train always won in that contest. She took several deep breaths, pulling herself together with an effort.

She couldn't think about this right now, she just couldn't. It was possible she had flu, nothing more. She had to stop jumping to conclusions. She'd been through a lot of stress lately. Far more stress than the average person had to deal with. There were plenty of reasons for her period to be late. And it wasn't really late. She could get her period any day now.

But the nagging fear wouldn't leave her alone.

She used the facilities and then splashed cold water on her face in a vain attempt to bring some color back to her cheeks. She stopped in the staff lounge to rummage for some crackers to nibble on as she made her way back to the trauma bay.

The pager at her waist beeped. She glanced at the display. *Thirty-five-year-old white male with multiple crushing injuries to torso and lower extremities. Intubated in the field, transfusing four units of O negative blood. ETA five minutes.*

Five minutes. She took another sip of white soda and finished the cracker. She couldn't decide if she should be upset or relieved when the cracker and white soda combination helped settle her stomach.

"What's wrong?" Caleb demanded when she entered the trauma bay a few moments later. "You look awful."

"Gee, thanks so much," she said sarcastically. "I really needed to hear that."

"I'm sorry, but I wanted to make sure that you're okay to work," Caleb amended. "The trauma surgeon has requested a hot unload. We need to get up to the helipad, they're landing in two minutes."

"I'm okay to work," she repeated firmly, determined to prove it by not falling apart as she had last night. Every day was better than the last one—hadn't her counselor stressed the importance of moving forward? She was living proof the strategy worked. "Let's go."

She and Caleb took the trauma elevators, located in the back of the trauma bay, up to the helipad on the roof of the hospital. At first the confines of the elevator bothered her, but she inhaled the heady scent of Caleb's aftershave, which pushed the bad memories away and reminded her of happier times. When they reached the helipad, they found the trauma surgeon, Dr. Eric Sutton, was already standing there, waiting. Lifting her hand to shield her eyes against the glare of the sun, Raine watched as the air-rescue chopper approached. The noise of the aircraft made it impossible to speak.

When the helicopter landed, they waited until they saw the signal from the pilot to approach, ducking well below the blades. The Lifeline transport team, consisting of a physician and a nurse, helped lift the patient out of the back hatch of the chopper.

"He's in bad shape, losing blood fast," the Lifeline physician grimly informed them. "In my opinion, you need to take him directly to the OR."

"Sounds like a plan. We can finish resuscitating him there," Dr. Sutton agreed. "Let's go."

In her year of working Trauma, she'd only transported a handful of patients directly to the OR. They all squeezed into the trauma elevator around the patient, Greg Hanson. She kept her gaze on the portable monitor, trying to ignore the close confines of the elevator as they rode back down to the trauma OR suite located on the second floor, directly above the ED.

The elevators opened into the main hallway of the OR. The handed the gurney over to the OR staff who were waiting, taking precious moments to don sterile garb before following the patient into the room.

"Caleb, I need a central line in this guy—he needs at least four more units of O neg blood," Sutton said.

They fell into a trauma resuscitation rhythm, only this time the trauma surgeon had taken the lead instead of Caleb. As Eric Sutton was assessing the extent of the patient's crushing leg wounds, she and Caleb worked together to get Greg Hanson's blood pressure up to a reasonable level.

She didn't know the circumstances about why Greg Hanson's car had been on the railroad tracks and as she hung four more units of blood on the rapid infusor, she found herself hoping this hadn't been a suicide attempt.

Being in close proximity to Caleb put all her senses on alert. But when his shoulders brushed against hers, she didn't flinch. She tried to see that as a sign she was healing.

"Here," she said, handing him the end of the rapid infuser tubing once he'd gotten the central line placed. "Connect this so I can get the blood started."

Caleb took the tubing from her hands, his fingers warm against hers. Eric and the OR nurse were prepping the patient's legs to begin surgery and the anesthesiologist was already putting the patient to sleep, but for a fraction of a second their gazes clung, as if they were all alone in the room.

"Great. All set," Caleb said, breaking the nearly tangible connection. "Start the blood."

She turned on the rapid infuser, rechecking the lines to make sure everything was properly connected. She took four more units of blood, confirmed the numbers matched, and then set them aside to be hung as soon as the other four had been transfused into their patient. She could see by the amount of blood already filling the large suction canisters that he was going to need more.

"Draw a full set of labs, Raine," Caleb told her.

She did as he asked, handing them over to the anesthesia tech, who ran them to the stat lab. She began hanging the new units of blood when the current bags were dry.

"I think we have things under control here," the anesthesiologist informed them a few minutes later. Taking a peek over the sterile drape, she could see Dr. Sutton was already in the process of repairing a torn femoral artery.

She was loath to leave, feeling as if there was still more they could do. But now that the anesthesiologist had put the patient to sleep, he'd taken over monitoring the rapid infuser, along with the anesthesia tech.

They really weren't needed here any longer.

Caleb put a hand on her arm, and she glanced up at him. The warmth in his gaze made it seem as if the last four weeks of being apart hadn't happened. "Come on, we need to get back down to the trauma bay."

"All right," she agreed, following him out of the OR suite. Outside the room, they stripped off the sterile garb covering their scrubs.

"Good work, Raine," Caleb told her, as they headed down to the trauma bay.

"Thanks. You too," she murmured, sending him a sideways glance. From the first time she'd met Caleb, there had been an undeniable spark between them. An awareness that had only intensified as they'd worked together.

His kisses had made her head spin. There was so much about him that she'd admired. And a few qualities she didn't.

Working together just now to save Greg Hanson's life had only reinforced how in sync they were. They made a great team.

Professional team, not a personal one, she reminded herself.

The nauseous feeling returned and she glanced away, feeling hopelessly desperate.

Impossible to go back and change the mistakes and subsequent events of the past, no matter how much she wished she could.

Caleb couldn't seem to keep his gaze off Raine. The adrenalin rush that came from helping to save a patient's life seemed to make everything around him stand out in sharp definition. Especially her. Raine's dark red hair, her pale skin, her bright blue eyes had beckoned to him from the moment they'd met.

She was so beautiful. His fingers itched to stroke her skin. Memories of how sweetly she'd responded to his kisses flooded his mind. Along with a stab of regret. If only he'd have handled things differently, they might have been able to make their relationship work.

His fault. She'd pushed him away, but it was all his fault. Because he'd jumped to conclusions.

Raine had tried to talk to him, but he hadn't been very receptive. And then Jake had come to apologize. Confessing that he'd had too much to drink and had made a pass at Raine.

So he'd called her back, prepared to apologize, but she'd refused to take his calls.

He wished, more than anything, that she'd talk to him. Allow him to clear things up between them. But instead she'd gone to work in the minor care area, located at the opposite end of the ED from the trauma bay.

He and Raine made a great team on a professional level. He shouldn't dwell on the fact they couldn't seem to make the same connection on a personal one.

"Where's my brother? Greg Hanson?" a frantic voice asked, as they walked past the ED patient waiting area.

Caleb stopped to address the young man. "He's in surgery. We can let the trauma surgeon, Dr. Eric Sutton, know you're here waiting for him."

"Surgery?" The man's expression turned hopeful. "So he's going to make it?"

"I'm sorry, but it's a little too early to say for sure, although I think he has a good fighting chance," Caleb told him. He glanced at Raine, who gave a nod of encouragement.

"His vital signs were stabilizing when we left," she added.

"Good, that's good." The young man sighed. "Greg's wife and baby are being examined to make sure they didn't sustain any injuries. He risked his life to save them. His wife, Lora, panicked when her van got stuck on the railroad tracks. She didn't want to leave because the baby was in the back seat. He pulled her out of the car first, and then yanked the baby out just as the train hit."

He heard Raine's soft gasp. "Dear heavens," she murmured.

Caleb grimly agreed. The guy was a hero, and he could only hope the poor guy didn't suffer irreparable damage to his legs as a result of his actions. "Are his wife and baby both here?"

"The baby's at Children's Memorial, my wife is over

there with their daughter now. Lora's here, the doctor is seeing her now. As soon as they're medically cleared, we'll all be here waiting to hear about Greg's condition."

"I'll let the trauma surgeon know," Caleb promised.

"Thank you," the young man said gratefully.

He and Raine returned to the trauma bay. He made the call up to the OR, leaving a message with the OR circulating nurse about Greg's family. She passed the word on to Eric Sutton, who reassured them he'd come to the waiting room to talk to the family as soon as he was finished.

Satisfied, he hung up the phone. There was a lull in the action. Trauma was either busy or slow, and he found himself looking once again for Raine.

They needed to talk. He just couldn't let her go without a fight. Maybe it was crazy, but the awareness still shimmering between them made him believe in second chances.

He found her in the staff lounge, sipping a soda. She looked surprised to see him.

"I was surprised to see you earlier today. You never mentioned working at the animal shelter while we were going out," he said, being careful to sound casual and not accusatory.

She met his gaze briefly, before glancing away. "No, I didn't. I've only been volunteering at the animal shelter for the past month or so."

The past month. Since their break-up. For some reason, the timing bothered him.

"Your dad is a sweetheart," she continued, staring down into the depths of her soft drink. "He's a great vet, really wonderful with animals. Everyone at the shelter loves him."

Strange, Raine had never struck him as being an animal lover, although now that he knew she was, he wondered what else he hadn't known about her.

And why did it matter now?

"Yeah, my dad has quite the female fan club," he said dryly. "Just ask any of his ex-wives."

She frowned at him and he immediately felt guilty for the lame joke.

"My dad is a great guy," he amended. "He does have a special talent for working with animals."

Raine nodded thoughtfully. And then she suddenly jumped to her feet. "Look, Caleb, I'm sorry things didn't work out between us on a personal level. But at least we know we can work together, right? We helped save Greg's life. Surely that counts for something."

Her words gave him the opportunity he needed.

"Raine, I'm sorry. I shouldn't have accused you of seeing Jake behind my back."

She stared at him with wide blue eyes. "Why were you so ready to believe the worst?" she asked in a low voice.

He swallowed hard, knowing she deserved the truth. "I had a bad experience with being cheated on in the past," he finally admitted. "I walked in and found my fiancée in bed with another man."

"I see." She frowned and broke away from his gaze.

Did she? He doubted it. "Look, Raine, I know now that I overreacted. Jake explained everything."

She brought her gaze, full of reproach, up to his. "So did I, remember? The next day, when I called you?"

He didn't know what to say to that, because what she said was the truth. She had tried to explain, but he hadn't believed her.

"You listened to Jake, but you didn't listen to me," Raine murmured, her blue eyes shadowed with pain. "I guess that sums everything up right there."

Panic gripped him by the throat. "Raine, please. Give me another chance."

She sighed and rubbed her temples. "It's too late, Caleb. There were a lot of other signs that you didn't trust me, but I tried to ignore them. The way you kept asking me where I was going and who I was going to be with. The night with Jake only solidified what I already knew."

"I learned my lesson," he quickly protested. "I promise, this time I'll trust you."

But she was already shaking her head. "It's not that easy, Caleb. Trust comes from within. You have to believe with your whole heart."

His whole heart? Her words nagged at him. Because he cared about Raine a lot. But had he loved her? He'd thought things were heading in that direction, but now he wasn't so sure.

Those feelings of intense betrayal, when he'd seen her with Jake, had haunted him. Had made him think the worst about her.

He remembered how Raine had tried to explain how thrilled and relieved she'd been to be away from the overbearing scrutiny of her three older brothers. At first she'd teasingly accused him of being just like them.

But then she'd become more resentful.

And he'd accused her of cheating on him.

No wonder she'd wanted a break.

Still, he wanted another chance. Even though there was something different about her. A shadow in her eyes that hadn't been there before. The Raine he'd worked with tonight didn't seem to be the same person she'd been a month earlier.

Because of him?

Caleb's stomach twisted with regret. He hadn't told her about his mother abandoning him and his father, taking off to follow her dream of being a dancer. Or the string of stepmothers and almost stepmothers. Obviously, he should have.

"Raine, I'm sorry. I know I don't deserve another chance, but—" He stopped when their pagers went off simultaneously.

Sixty-nine-year-old male passed out at home, pulse irregular and slow, complaining of new onset chest pain. ETA three minutes.

"How about we focus on being friends?" she said. "Excuse me, but I need to make sure everything is ready for our new patient." Raine brushed past him to head towards the trauma room.

He followed more slowly, watching as Raine and Sarah double-checked the equipment and supplies they had on standby.

They didn't have to wait long. When the doors from the paramedic bay burst open, he was assailed by a strange sense of déjà vu as the paramedic crew wheeled in their new arrival.

Raine's sudden gasp made him frown. And in the next second he understood as he recognized the patient too.

His father.

CHAPTER FOUR

RAINE glanced at Caleb, worried about his reaction. She couldn't imagine how it would feel to have your father being wheeled into the trauma bay.

She grabbed the closest ED tech. "Ben, run to the arena and ask Dr. Garrison to come over." She stepped up to put the elderly vet on the heart monitor. Caleb couldn't function as his father's physician. Especially when Dr. Frank's face was sweaty and pale, his eyes closed and his facial muscles drawn, as if he was in extreme pain.

Caleb surprised her by stepping up and taking control. "He's still bradycardic. Raine, start oxygen at two liters per minute. Send a cardiac injury panel and then we'll run a twelve-lead EKG."

"He'll need something for pain, too." The paramedic had placed the oxygen on, so she concentrated on drawing blood, knowing they needed the results stat in order to determine if he should go straight to the cardiac cath lab. But Dr. Frank's pain was her next priority.

"Dr. Garrison can't come," Ben announced when he returned from the arena, a tad short of breath himself. "He's about to deliver a baby."

"A baby?" Raine echoed in shocked amazement. Good grief, could things get any worse? She shot a quick glance at Caleb before giving his father two milligrams of morphine. And then called for the EKG tech.

"I'm fine," Caleb said in a low tone, answering her unspoken question. "We're going to need to call the cardiologist anyway, since I'm sure my father is having an acute myocardial infarct."

"Can't you…just call it…a heart attack?" his father asked in a feebly sarcastic tone.

"Dr. Frank, you need to try to relax," Raine urged, putting a reassuring hand on his arm. "We don't know for sure that you're having a heart attack, but we're going to do all the preliminary tests just in case."

The vet ignored her, his gaze locked on his son. "I should have…told you."

Raine glanced up at Caleb, who'd come up to stand beside his father. She continued to record vital signs as they spoke.

"Should have told me what?" Caleb asked urgently. "Have you had chest pain before?"

"No. Dizzy spells." Caleb's father spoke in short phrases, his breathing still labored. Raine cranked up the oxygen to five liters per minute as his pulse ox reading was only 89 percent. "I got dizzy-and fell off…the ladder."

Caleb's breath hissed out between his teeth. But his tone was surprisingly gentle. "Yes, you should have told me."

"Denial…can be…very powerful." His father's eyes were shadowed with regret.

Raine stepped in with a bright smile, trying to ease the tension between father and son. "Well, thank heavens you're here now. Don't worry, Dr. Frank, we're going to take good care of you."

"You're…a sweet girl…Raine."

Caleb's smile was strained. "Dad, Geoff Lyons is the cardiologist on call, he should be here to see you shortly. How's your chest pain? Any better?"

"Not much," his dad answered.

"Raine, start him on a nitroglycerine drip. If that doesn't help, we'll give him another two milligrams of morphine."

She was already crossing over to the pharmaceutical dispensing machine to fetch a bottle of nitroglycerine and more morphine.

The phone rang and she could hear Caleb crossing over to answer it. She listened as he repeated the critical troponin level of 2.4 and gave his name before hanging up.

His father was more alert than he let on. "Guess I've…earned a trip…to the cath lab."

"Yes." Caleb glanced up in relief when Dr. Geoff Lyons walked in.

"What's going on?" Geoff asked.

Raine gave Dr. Frank more morphine as Caleb and Geoff discussed the results of the EKG and the lab work. She stayed by his side as Dr. Lyons made arrangements for Caleb's dad to be transferred to the cardiac cath lab.

"You'll be fine," Raine told him reassuringly, as she connected him to the transport monitor.

"I'll see you after the procedure, Dad," Caleb added.

"Caleb…take care of Grizz for me," his father whispered.

"I will. I'll run and get him after my shift." Caleb squeezed his father's hand and then stepped back.

"Is there someone else we should call?" Raine asked him softly, as the cardiac team whisked Caleb's dad away. "Your mom? Brothers or sisters?"

"No." Caleb gave a deep sigh. "My dad isn't married at the moment and he's recently broken up with his current lady friend, Sharon. My mother took off years ago, and she has her own family now."

The way he spoke of his mother, so matter-of-fact, wrenched her heart. He'd never mentioned his mother leaving before. What sort of mother abandoned her son? No wonder Caleb found it hard to believe in women. "I'm sorry," she said helplessly.

"Not your fault." Caleb brushed her sympathy aside as if determined to make her believe he was over it. "We'd better get ready for the next patient."

"The next patient?" She stared at him as if he'd lost his mind. "Caleb, your father is having a heart procedure. I'm sure one of the physicians would be willing to cover for you."

"I'm fine. There's nothing I can do until after his procedure is over anyway." His dark, stormy gray eyes warned her not to say anything more, before he turned and walked away.

Caleb was determined to finish his shift, even though his thoughts kept straying to his father.

He didn't blame his dad for not telling him about the dizzy spells. Rather, he was upset with himself. He should have forced his father to go in to be checked out when he'd fallen off the ladder in the first place.

If he'd have listened to his gut instinct, it was possible

he could have prevented the additional damage to his father's heart.

He could feel Raine's concerned gaze following him as they worked on their next patient, an abdominal stabbing sustained during a bar fight. The tip of the blade had just missed the diaphragm, which was lucky as that meant his breathing wasn't impaired, but Caleb was certain either the stomach or the intestines had been hit.

"Raine, we need to explore the depth of the wound," he informed her.

She nodded her understanding and quickly began prepping the area with antimicrobial solution before spreading several sterile drapes around the wound. Once he'd donned his sterile gear, he reached for a scalpel. "Hold the retractor for me, will you? Like this."

She did as he asked, opening the wound so he could see better. The damage wasn't as bad as he'd expected, although the laceration in the small intestine meant the patient would need surgery. He irrigated the wound with sterile saline to help clean it out. "Okay, that's all we can do here. Put a dressing over this, would you? I need to get in touch with the general surgeon on call. This guy needs a small bowel resection."

Once he'd gotten their stab patient transferred to the care of the general surgeon, he checked his watch, wondering how his father was doing. A good hour had passed since he'd been taken up to the cardiac cath lab.

"Caleb? There's a phone call for you." Raine's expression was troubled as she handed him the receiver.

The display on the phone indicated the call was from

the OR, not the cath lab. Was this regarding his stab-wound patient? "This is Dr. Stewart."

"Caleb, it's Geoff Lyons. I'm sorry to tell you that your father's condition took a turn for the worse. We had to abort the attempt to place a stent. I called a cardiothoracic surgeon in for assistance. Dr. Summers has taken him to the OR for three-vessel cardiac bypass surgery."

Raine watched the blood drain from Caleb's face and feared the news wasn't good. When he hung up the phone, she crossed over to him. "What's wrong? Your father?"

"In the OR, having cardiac bypass surgery." Caleb's expression was grim. "They couldn't get the stent placed and his condition grew very unstable, so they called in the surgeon."

"I'm sorry," she murmured, feeling helpless. "Do you want me to call Dr. Garrison to cover you? There's only about an hour and a half left of the shift."

"I'll talk to him," Caleb said. She was somewhat surprised he'd given in. Of course, there was a huge difference between having a cardiac cath procedure and full-blown open-heart surgery.

Dr. Joe Garrison agreed to cover and luckily the steady stream of trauma calls seemed to dwindle. At the end of her shift, she transferred her last patient to the ICU and then was free to go.

Raine couldn't bring herself to head home, though. Instead, after she swiped out, she went to the OR waiting room to find Caleb.

He was sitting with his elbows propped on his knees,

his head cradled in his hands. He looked so alone, she was glad she'd come.

"Hey," she said, dropping into the seat beside him. "Have you heard anything?"

He lifted his head to look at her, his forehead furrowed with lines of exhaustion. "Not really, other than a quick call to let me know this could take hours yet. Is your shift over already?"

"Yes, and don't worry, it was relatively quiet. Not a problem at all for Dr. Garrison to cover."

Caleb nodded. "I'm glad. I was just thinking about whether or not I should leave for a while to pick up Grizz. I'm sure he'll need to go outside soon."

"I can run and let him out if you like," she offered. "I'd take him home with me, but my apartment doesn't allow dogs."

"Thanks, but I need to get him moved into my house anyway, now that Dad's going to be in the hospital for a while." Caleb rubbed the back of his neck and slowly stood.

She stared at him, wondering about this sudden urge to pick up the dog. Was he looking for an excuse to get away from her?

And, really, could she blame him? He'd asked for a second chance, but she'd refused.

But they could still be friends, couldn't they?

"Do you want some company?" she asked lightly.

He hesitated for a moment, and then nodded. "Sure."

Okay, so maybe Caleb wasn't looking for an excuse to avoid her. She had to stop second-guessing his motives. She stood and followed him to the parking structure where all the ED employees parked. "Do you want me to drive?"

He shook his head. "I'll drive."

She wasn't surprised—her brothers would have said the exact same thing. She didn't understand the macho need to drive, but figured it had something to do with wanting to be in control. She slid into the passenger seat, remembering the last time she'd ridden with Caleb.

On their last date before the Jake fiasco. A romantic dinner and a trip to the theater to see *Phantom of the Opera*. She'd never enjoyed herself more.

Regret twisted like a knife in her heart.

Caleb didn't say anything on the short ride to his father's house. She pushed aside her own tangled emotions, understanding that at this moment, Caleb was deeply worried about his father. And she certainly couldn't blame him.

She was worried too.

"Your dad is strong, Caleb. He's going to pull through this just fine."

He glanced at her and nodded. "I know. It's just..." His voice trailed off.

"What?" she asked.

He let out a heavy sigh. "My dad and I don't see eye-to-eye on a lot of things, but that doesn't mean I don't love him. I just wish I would have told him that before he left to go to the cardiac cath lab. I should have said the words."

Her heart squeezed in her chest. She reached out to lightly touch his arm. "He knows, Caleb. Your dad knows how much you love him."

He didn't respond, but pulled into his father's driveway. She'd been there earlier that day, when she'd driven Dr. Frank home from the animal shelter. He got out of the car and she followed him into the dark house.

"Hi, Grizz." Caleb smiled a bit when the dog greeted them enthusiastically, trying to lick both of them in his excitement to see them.

"Grizz, you're just a big old softie, aren't you?" Raine said, stroking his wiggling body.

"Will you take him out into the back yard for me?" Caleb asked. "I need to get all his stuff packed into the car as he's coming home with me."

"Sure. Come on, Grizz," she called, walking through the house, flicking on lights as she went. The back door was in the kitchen, and she followed the dog outside, waiting patiently while he took care of business.

He bounded toward her soon afterwards and she stroked his silky fur. "I bet you're already missing Dr. Frank, aren't you?" she murmured. "Don't worry, I'm sure Caleb is going to take good care of you."

She took Grizz back inside the house to find Caleb lugging a forty-pound bag of dog food out to his car.

"All set?" she asked as he closed the trunk.

"Yes." He opened the back passenger door. "Come on, Grizz, you get the whole back seat to yourself."

The ride to Caleb's house didn't take long and when she followed him inside, she was assaulted by memories. Good memories. Painfully good memories. She averted her gaze from the sofa where she and Caleb had very nearly made love.

She wished more than ever she'd made love to Caleb that night. Now it was too late.

She put a hand to her stomach, surprised to note her earlier attack of nausea seemed to have gone away. Determined to hope for the best, she told herself that was a good thing. Maybe the sickness was nothing more than a touch of flu.

Grizz paced around Caleb's house, sniffing at everything with interest. When he'd finished exploring his new surroundings, and apparently deemed them acceptable, he made himself comfortable by flopping on Caleb's sofa.

She heard Caleb sigh, but he didn't make Grizz get down. Instead, he reached over to scratch the silky fur behind his ears. "I'll be back later, Grizz, okay?"

The dog thumped his tail on the sofa in agreement.

Raine followed Caleb back outside to his car. The ride back to the hospital was quiet.

When he'd parked the car, he turned toward her. "Thanks for coming with me, Raine."

"You're welcome." She tilted her head curiously, wondering if he was wanting to get rid of her. "Ready to head inside to see if there's any news on your dad?"

He took the key from the ignition and flashed a tired smile. "Raine, it's well after midnight. I appreciate everything you've done, but I'm sure you're exhausted. It's fine if you'd rather head home."

Slowly she shook her head. No matter what had transpired between her and Caleb in the past, there was no way in the world she could just walk away. Not now. She opened her passenger side door with determination. "Let's find out how he's doing, okay? Then I'll head home."

Caleb didn't protest when she followed him inside, riding the elevator up to the waiting room. She wanted to believe he was glad to have her around, but suspected he was just too tired to argue.

The desk in the waiting room was empty. Apparently the volunteers who usually manned the area had already gone home for the night.

She stood off to the side, while Caleb picked up the phone to call up to the OR.

"This is Caleb Stewart. Is there any news on my father, Frank Stewart?"

Raine couldn't hear what was said on the other end of the line, but when Caleb nodded and murmured thanks, before hanging up, she couldn't help asking, "Is he still in surgery?"

"Yeah. They're finished with the main portion of the procedure, and they're starting to close him now. They estimate he'll be in the ICU within the hour."

The knotted muscles in her neck eased. "That's good news."

"Yeah, although apparently he ended up having his aortic valve replaced too, in addition to the repairs to his coronary arteries." Caleb scrubbed a hand over his face. "But he's hanging in there, so I'm going to keep hoping for the best."

She watched as he crossed over to take a seat. He glanced up in surprise when she followed. "Raine, I don't expect you to hang out here with me indefinitely."

They may have dated for two months, but he obviously didn't know her very well. Why was he so anxious to believe the worst about her? Just because he'd been cheated on in the past? Was it possible he was incapable of trusting her at all? Maybe. But no matter what had transpired between them, she couldn't have left him alone in that waiting room if her life had depended on it.

She dropped into the seat beside him, curling her legs underneath her. "I'm not leaving, Caleb. I'm staying."

CHAPTER FIVE

C<small>ALEB</small> glanced over at Raine sitting in the waiting-room chair, her eyes closed as she'd finally given in to her exhaustion. He stared at her, watching her sleep, trying to figure her out.

After not seeing her for the past month, it was scary how easily they'd ended up here together. He almost reached out to brush a strand of hair away from her eyes, but stopped himself just in time. He didn't want to read too much into her actions, but he couldn't help from wondering if her staying here with him meant she was willing to give him another chance.

And would he mess things up again, if she did?

He let out a heavy sigh, wishing he knew the answer to that one. Raine was beautiful, smart and funny. He'd enjoyed just being with her. But he couldn't blame the demise of their relationship solely on her. He owned a big piece of the problem.

Trust didn't come easy. And he didn't have a clue how to fix the tiny part of him that always held back. The tiny part of him that always doubted.

The tiny part of him that constantly expected and saw the worst.

The door to the waiting room swung open, distracting him from his reverie. An older man dressed in scrubs, a surgical mask dangling around his neck, emerged through the doorway. He recognized him as Dr. Steve Summers, one of the cardiothoracic surgeons who operated out of Trinity Medical Center.

"Raine?" Caleb reached over to gently shake her shoulder to wake her up.

At his touch, she bolted upright and recoiled from him, her eyes wide and frightened as she frantically looked around the room. "What?"

He frowned, bothered by her reaction. Had he interrupted a bad dream? He gestured to the CT surgeon who was approaching. "The doctor is here."

"Caleb Stewart?" the cardiothoracic surgeon asked, as he crossed over to shake his hand. "Steve Summers. I thought your name was familiar. I recognize you from the ED. Your father has been transferred to the ICU. I had to replace his aortic valve along with three of his coronary arteries. His heart took a bad hit and he lost a fair amount of blood, but seems to be holding his own at the moment."

Caleb knew that was a tactful way of saying his father was still in a critical condition. He'd used the same lines with family members himself. "How long do you think he'll need to stay in the ICU?"

"At least a day or two." Steve glanced curiously at Raine, no doubt recognizing her too, but then turned back to Caleb. "If he stays stable over the next couple of hours, I'll take him off the ventilator. The sooner we can get him breathing on his own, the shorter his recovery time should be."

"Can Caleb go up to see him?" Raine asked.

"Sure. Just give the nurses a couple of minutes to get things settled, and then you can head up." The surgeon flashed a tired smile. "I'm sure he's going to do just fine."

Caleb wished he could be as sure, but he nodded anyway and shook the surgeon's hand gratefully. "Thanks again."

The surgeon returned the handshake before turning to leave. He glanced at Raine. "Do you want to come upstairs to the ICU with me?"

She hesitated, her arms crossed defensively over her chest, her expression uncertain. "I'd be happy to come up if you like, but I don't want to intrude. He's your father. I'm just an acquaintance."

The way she backed off made him question her motives for staying in the first place. Maybe this was her way of telling him she was willing to be there for him, but only up to a point? She had told him they should just try being friends. It was possible she didn't want to come along because they weren't formally dating.

He swallowed the urge to ask her to come along, respecting the distance she apparently wanted to keep. Especially considering Raine had already gone above and beyond, sitting here with him while he'd waited to hear how his father had fared. Besides, it was already two in the morning and he understood she needed to get home. "Are you sure you're okay to drive?" he asked instead.

"Absolutely. I'm awake now." Her lopsided smile

tugged at his heart. "Tell your dad I'm thinking about him and that he needs to get better soon, all right?"

"Sure." His fingers itched to touch her, to pull her close, seeking comfort in her warm embrace. But they were colleagues. Maybe even friends. Nothing more. "Take care."

"You too, Caleb," she said softly.

They left the waiting room together, but then parted ways, heading in opposite directions. For a long moment, he watched her heading toward the parking structure, fighting the desperate need to call her back.

Cursing himself for being a fool, he turned away, heading toward the elevator to go up to the critical care unit.

It felt strange to walk into the busy unit as a visitor rather than as a physician. When he approached his father's room, his footsteps slowed.

As a doctor, he'd known what to expect. But seeing his dad so pale, connected to all the machinery, it made his breath lodge in his throat. He took a moment to watch his father's vital signs roll across the screen on the monitor hanging over his bed. The numbers were reassuring, so he softly approached his father's bedside.

The bitter taste of regret filled his mouth. He reached down and took his father's hand in his. "I love you, Dad," he whispered.

His father's eyes fluttered open, his gaze locking on his. Caleb blinked away the dampness of tears and leaned forward, holding his father's gaze. "The surgery is over and you're doing fine, Dad," he assured him, knowing his father couldn't speak with the breathing tube in his throat. "I took Grizz to my house, so you don't need to worry about a thing. Just rest and get better soon, okay?"

His father nodded and then his eyes drifted shut, as if that brief interaction had been all he could manage. Caleb squeezed his father's hand again, and then slowly released it.

Part of him wanted to stay, but there was really no purpose. In fact, he had to get home to take care of Grizz, as he'd promised. His father needed to rest, anyway. There was nothing more he could do here.

Regretfully, he turned away. His dad was a fighter. He was sure his dad would feel better in the morning.

Caleb went home, surprisingly glad when Grizzly dashed over to greet him. He hadn't realized what a difference it made to come home to a pet rather than an empty house.

"Hey, Grizz, were you afraid I wasn't coming back?" He scratched the dog behind the ears. He let the dog outside and then made his way into the bedroom. Grizz followed, tail wagging, glancing around the new environment.

"I bet you miss him, don't you, boy?" Caleb murmured. Grizzly laid his head on the edge of the bed, staring up at him with large soulful brown eyes. "I know. I miss him, too."

It was true, he realized. He did miss his father. But, truth be told, he missed what he and Raine had once had together even more.

Raine had the next day off, so she didn't see either Caleb or Dr. Frank. But she called the ICU and was told Caleb's father was in serious but stable condition. Raine knew if she wanted more details, she'd have to ask Caleb.

Or visit Dr. Frank for herself.

She kept busy at the animal shelter, glad to see the animals were doing much better. Everyone was concerned about Dr. Frank, so she told them enough to satisfy their curiosity without violating his privacy.

The next day, Friday, she was scheduled to work, so she went to the hospital an hour early to sneak up to Dr. Frank's room for a quick visit. Normally, the ICU only allowed immediate family members to come up, but her hospital ID badge worked to open the doors so she was able to walk in.

She found Caleb's father's room easily enough.

"Hi, Raine," Dr. Frank greeted her with a tired smile. "How are you? How are things at the shelter?"

"They're fine. In fact, I brought you pictures. See?" She took several glossy photos out of her purse and spread them out over his bedside table, knowing he'd appreciate them more than a handful of balloons and a sappy card. "Rusty, Annie, Ace and Maggie all miss you."

Dr. Frank's smile widened when he saw the pictures of his favorite dogs at the shelter. There were dozens of animals at the shelter, but since she couldn't take pictures of them all, she'd focused on the dogs who'd been sick, so he could see how much better they were doing. "They're beautiful, Raine. Thanks. I wish I had a picture of Grizzly, too."

"I'm sure Caleb is taking good care of him," she said reassuringly. No matter how much Dr. Frank missed his dog, there was no way she was going to ask Caleb if she could stop by to take a picture of Grizz.

That would be taking their new-found fragile truce a little too far.

"He is. I just miss him," Dr. Frank said in a wistful tone.

"Everyone at the shelter hopes you get better soon. I didn't tell them much, only that you were in the hospital and doing fine."

The older man lifted a narrow shoulder. "I don't mind if they know about my surgery. Seems like they'll figure out something is wrong when I'm not able to work for several weeks."

"Okay, I'll let them know. When are you getting out of here?" Raine asked, changing the subject with a quick glance around his room. "I thought they were transferring you out of the ICU to a regular floor sometime soon."

"That's the plan." Dr. Frank's gaze focused on something past her shoulder so she turned round, in time to see Caleb walking into the room. Her heart lurched a bit in her chest but he wasn't smiling. She hadn't seen him in the past twenty-four hours, and had no idea why he might be upset.

Her stomach churned, the nausea that came and went seemingly at will, returning with a vengeance. Since the nausea hadn't been as bad over the past day or so, she'd convinced herself the sensation had been nothing more than her over-active imagination. Or a touch of flu.

Now she wasn't so sure. Suddenly her stomach hurt so badly she could barely stand upright. She swallowed hard and prayed she wouldn't throw up her breakfast.

Fighting for control, she pushed away the desperate fear and worry. Enough playing the denial game. She needed to stop avoiding the possibility. She'd go and buy a stupid pregnancy test so that she knew for sure what was going on.

Everything inside her recoiled at the thought of being pregnant.

"Hi, Dad, you look much better today," Caleb said, crossing over to his father's bedside. He frowned a little when he glanced at Raine. "Are you all right?"

"Fine," she forced herself to answer cheerfully, when she felt anything but. Of course he'd noticed something was wrong. She wished Caleb was a little less observant. "Just hungry. I didn't eat anything for lunch. I'm going to get going now, so I can eat before my shift." She knew she was babbling, but didn't care. She wanted to get out of there, fast. "Take care, Dr. Frank, I'll let everyone at the shelter know you're doing better."

"All right. Thanks for the pictures, Raine." Caleb's dad looked better, but it was obvious he still tired easily. Just her short visit seemed to have worn him out.

She edged toward the door. "Bye, Caleb."

"See you later," he said as she practically ran from the room.

Raine sought refuge in the nearest ladies room, bending over and clutching her stomach until the urge to throw up passed. She didn't have time now, before work, but she was going to have to get a home pregnancy test soon.

Tonight.

And if it was positive, she'd deal with that news the

same way she'd dealt with everything else that had happened.

Alone.

Raine was glad she was able to avoid the trauma room for her Friday night shift. The patients seen in the arena certainly needed care, but it wasn't the life-and-death action that the trauma bay held.

But moving to the arena didn't help her escape Caleb.

"You're working tonight?" she asked, when he walked in, hoping her dismay didn't show. The nausea she'd felt earlier hadn't gone away.

Caleb shrugged. "I'll need to take some time off once my dad is discharged from the hospital, so I figured I should work now."

Since his logic made sense, she couldn't argue. "He seems to be doing much better," Raine said.

"Yeah, he is." Caleb raked his fingers through his hair. "I guess they bumped me out of Trauma for tonight. Brock Madison is covering the trauma bay instead."

Probably in deference to what he was going through with his dad. Something she should have figured out for herself, before switching to work in the arena.

Elana had called off sick, so they were a little short-handed, but Raine didn't mind. If she could find a way to keep her emotions under control and her stomach from rebelling, she'd be fine.

Their sickest patient was a woman with congestive heart failure, who'd been taken into the arena when she'd first arrived, but then had quickly needed more care. They would have moved her to the trauma bay, except that they were busy with traumas, which meant they had to manage her here.

"Raine, have you sent the blood gases yet?" Caleb asked.

"Yes." She frowned, glancing at the clock. "The results should be back by now. I'll call the lab."

She made the phone call, gritting her teeth in frustration when the lab claimed they'd never got the specimen. She hung up the phone and turned toward Caleb. "The sample got lost in the tube system. I'll have to redraw it."

"That's fine." He kept his attention focused on the chart.

The night they'd saved Greg Hanson's life they'd been completely in sync. Now that companionable relationship seemed to have vanished. Her stomach lurched again, and she concentrated on drawing the arterial blood gas sample from Mrs. Jones, trying to ignore it.

"Yvonne?" she called out to the middle-aged female tech working on their team. "Will you run this to the lab? I don't want this one to get lost, too."

"Sure." Yvonne willingly took the blood tube from her hands.

"Thanks." She took another sip of her white soda, before logging into the system to document the latest set of vital signs. In the lull of waiting for the lab results, she escaped for a few minutes, seeking refuge in the staff lounge.

Closing her eyes, she tried to focus on staying calm. But the more her nausea plagued her, the more she tensed up. She took several deep breaths, pulled up her legs and rested her forehead on her knees.

She couldn't keep up the pretense much longer. She needed to know if she really was pregnant, and soon. She shouldn't have put it off as long as she already had. She should know by now that denial didn't work.

Hadn't Caleb's dad said something to that effect? About how denial was a powerful thing? After everything she'd gone through, she should know by now that denial was a death-trap. Better to face the things you were afraid of head-on.

Dr. Frank's heart attack had distracted her from her personal problems. Being with Caleb had certainly helped. She missed being with him, more than she'd ever imagined she would. Had she made a mistake in not confiding in him? Would their relationship have survived? Maybe. But even the thought of telling him made her nausea spike. No, it was better that she'd broken things off.

Her fault, not his. And there was no going back. Thinking about what might have been was nothing but foolish fantasy.

Even if Caleb could learn to trust her. Which was doubtful.

Especially now that the damage had been done.

"Raine?" Yvonne poked her head into the staff lounge. "There you are. Dr. Stewart is looking for you."

She pasted a smile on her face, hoping she didn't look as awful as she felt. "Okay, I'm coming."

Caleb glanced up when she approached. "We have her blood gases back and Margaret Jones needs to be transferred up to the medical ICU. You need to make the arrangements." His face was drawn into a slight scowl.

"Next time I'd appreciate you telling me who's covering while you're on break."

"I was only gone ten minutes," she snapped. The surge of anger was a welcome respite from soul-wrenching desperation. "But, rest assured, I'll be sure to tell you every time I need to use the restroom so you'll know exactly where I am."

He stared at her for a long moment, before he let out a heavy sigh. "You're right, I was out of line. I'm sorry. Just call up to give report, will you? Our patient in room two, Jerry Applegate, with sutures over his left eye, is also ready to be discharged. I need you to move fast. I'm being asked to clear our patients out as the waiting room is full."

His apology diffused her annoyance. She needed to pull herself together.

She didn't want to lose the collaborative working relationship she and Caleb had managed to maintain in spite of their break-up. Especially not when their friendship seemed a bit tenuous.

She worked quickly to get Mrs. Jones transferred up to the medical ICU. As soon as that transfer was completed, she discharged Jerry Applegate, the man who'd had a few too many beers at the local tavern and had fallen and cut his eye. He'd sobered up the moment Caleb had placed the first suture. She began to ask him about the possibility of alcoholism, but he mumbled something about a retirement party, looking so embarrassed she ended up giving him the teaching materials on the subject rather than her usual spiel before sending him on his way.

The disinfectant used to clean his room wasn't even dry when the triage nurse called.

"We have a female assault victim," the triage nurse informed her. "I'm bringing her back to room two right away."

Raine didn't remember dropping the phone, but soon she realized the buzzing in her ears was actually the phone beeping because it was off the hook. Glancing down, she saw it was lying on its side. She fumbled a bit with the effort of picking up the receiver and placing it back in its cradle.

A female assault victim. Her mind could barely comprehend the news. She took a deep breath and let it out slowly. Surely this wasn't the same circumstances. No, it was more likely a result of some sort of domestic dispute. Like poor Becca. Tragic, yes, but not the same situation at all.

Yet she couldn't seem to make her feet move. She couldn't do this. She couldn't. Her stomach tightened painfully. She needed to find someone else to care for the patient. Anyone. If only Elana hadn't called in sick, her friend would have taken over in a heartbeat.

"Raine?" Yvonne poked her head out from behind the doorway of room two, her eyes wide with compassion and alarm. "I need you. Right away."

Oh, God. A quick glance at the other teams in the arena proved everyone was busy. There was no one to take her place. Four weeks had passed but at this moment it seemed as if it had only been four days.

Dread seeped from her pores as Raine forced herself to walk into the room. A young woman, about her age, was seated on the hospital bed, clutching the edges of a blanket she'd wrapped tightly around herself.

Numbly, Raine took the clipboard Yvonne shoved into her hands and glanced at the paperwork. The girl's name was Helen Shore and she was twenty-five years old. Dragging her gaze back to her patient, she noted the girl looked disheveled, her blonde hair tangled up in knots, her face pale and her mascara smudged beneath her eyes.

Pure instinct and compassion took over. Ignoring her own feelings and the persistent nausea, she stepped forward, keeping her tone low and soothing as she addressed the patient. "Helen, my name is Raine, and I'm a nurse. Can you tell me what happened?"

The girl's eyes filled with tears. "I don't know what happened. I can't remember. *I can't remember!*"

"Shh, it's okay." Raine crossed over to put a supporting arm around the girl's shoulders. She knew, only too well, exactly how Helen felt. The void where your memory should have been threatened to swallow you whole. Her own horrific experience had happened a month ago, but she was suddenly reliving every detail.

She pushed the fears away, trying to keep focused on Helen. The girl was her patient. The poor young woman had come here for help. "Do you have bruises? Do you hurt anywhere?"

Helen nodded, tears making long black streaks on her cheeks. "When I woke up...my clothes were off. And...was hurt. I think—I might have been raped."

CHAPTER SIX

THE room spun dizzily and Raine's knees buckled. She grabbed the edge of the bed, holding herself upright out of sheer stubbornness. But her mind whirled, drawing parallels matching the horrific experience she'd endured with this poor girl's situation.

She swallowed hard and tried to gather her scattered thoughts. She needed to get a grip. This wasn't about her. She needed to focus on the patient. Helen.

"Yvonne, please find Dr. Stewart, will you?" Raine wasn't sure how she managed to sound so calm. "I need him to approve some orders."

"Of course." Yvonne ducked from the room.

Helen tightened her grip on the blanket, her eyes wide and frightened in her face. "Is Dr. Stewart a man? Because I don't want him to examine me unless he's a woman."

The disjointed protest didn't make much sense, but Raine understood exactly what Helen was trying to tell her.

"Dr. Stewart is a man, but he won't examine you," she explained gently. "We have nurses, female nurses, who have special training as sexual assault experts to do that. Dr. Stewart does need to write the orders, though.

We'll need to draw some blood so we can run lab tests, to see if you have any drugs in your system."

"Drugs? I don't do drugs. Oh..." Helen's face paled and her eyes filled with fresh tears. "You mean he gave me something? Is that why I can't remember?"

Rohypnol was the drug they'd found in her bloodstream. But there were various date-rape drugs on the streets. She'd spent hours searching through the information on the internet. Even alcohol could be used to encourage a woman to do something she normally wouldn't do.

There were plenty of men who would take advantage of the opportunity.

Her skin felt cold and clammy, and she tightened her grip on the edge of Helen's bed in an effort to keep her mind grounded in reality. Thankfully the patient was too traumatized to realize there was something wrong with her nurse. Raine tried to speak calmly through the dull roaring in her ears. "We won't know until we get the test results back. When did this happen?"

"Last night, late. We closed the bar. But I didn't wake up until a couple hours ago. I slept all day. I never sleep all day."

Most likely because of the drugs. Especially if they were mixed with something else. "And were you drinking alcohol, too?"

"Yes." Helen dropped her chin to her chest, as if she couldn't bear to make eye contact. "Cosmo martinis."

The potent beverage may have been enough, but Raine didn't think so. Helen's total lack of memory sounded more like a date-rape drug than just alcohol alone. Men used it specifically so that the women they preyed upon couldn't remember anything incriminating.

To hide the extent of their crime.

"We need to contact the police," Raine said softly, knowing Helen wasn't going to like having to retell her story to the authorities. She wanted to say something reassuring, but couldn't think of a thing.

She knew better than most, there was no easy way to get through everything facing Helen from this point forward. Especially if there were long-term ramifications, like becoming pregnant.

Her patient didn't have a chance to respond to the news because at that moment the glass door slid open and Caleb walked in.

"Dr. Stewart, this is Helen Shore," Raine said, maintaining her professionalism with an effort. "We believe she's been sexually assaulted. We need an order for a drug screen and the SANE nurse." She stared at a spot over his left ear, hoping he couldn't tell how she was barely hanging onto her composure.

"Already done," he said. "Yvonne filled me in and the SANE nurse has already arrived. As soon as you're ready for the exam, she'll come in."

Raine froze. Oh, God. No. There was no way she could stay, not for this. She forced herself to meet his gaze. "Will you ask Yvonne to accompany Helen during the exam?"

He flashed a puzzled look, but nodded. "Sure."

Thank heavens. Raine released her death grip on the bed and walked towards the door.

But she didn't quite make it to the opening before her world went black.

* * *

Caleb reached out and grabbed Raine, hauling her upright before she hit the floor.

She was out cold, her head lolling against the crook of his arm, her dark red hair and smattering of freckles creating a stark contrast against her pale skin.

"What the—?" He swung her limp body into his arms and carried her to the only open bed they had on their team, room five. There was a minor burn patient from the waiting room slotted to be admitted in there, but he didn't care. At the moment Raine took priority. Gently, he set her on the bed.

Within seconds her eyelids fluttered open and she stared up at him in confusion. "What happened?"

"You tell me," he muttered, his voice grim. He was glad she'd come round so quickly, but couldn't help the sharp flash of concern and annoyance at how she obviously wasn't taking very good care of herself. He hadn't liked the awful way she'd looked awful earlier in his dad's room and now this. "You fainted. When's the last time you had something to eat?"

She winced and avoided his direct gaze. "I… um…ate before my shift."

He didn't believe her. "Take a break. Now." Caleb dragged a hand through his hair. She'd taken ten years off his life when she'd crumpled like a rag doll.

"I'm fine," she protested, pushing up on her elbows to sit upright. She ran a hand over her forehead and he could see the faint sheen of sweat dampening her fingertips. Her pulse was racing and her blood pressure was probably non-existent. "I never faint."

"Could have fooled me," he said, stepping forward

to put a hand on her shoulder to keep her in place. "Give yourself a few minutes' rest before going back to work, would you? I'd rather arrange for someone to come in to give you a full physical exam. Please don't take this the wrong way, but you look like hell."

Her eyes widened in horror at the suggestion. "No. I'm fine. I don't want an exam."

"Raine." He stared at her until she met his gaze. "I'm not kidding. Tell me what's going on. What's wrong?"

"Nothing." She avoided his gaze in a way that made him grind his teeth in helpless frustration. Why wouldn't she open up to him? Talk to him? "I swear I just had a physical exam not too long ago. I'm fine."

He stared at her, willing her to open up about what was going on. But she sat up, swinging her legs over the edge of the bed as if to prove she was fine. "I'll be all right in a few minutes. In the meantime, I'll ask Ellen or Tracey to cover for me."

He couldn't force her to stay, but that didn't mean he was particularly happy when she stood on shaky legs. He stayed within reach, watching to make sure she didn't fall again.

It was ridiculous to be hurt by her decision. Raine couldn't have made her feelings any clearer. She didn't want or need his help.

There were no second chances. At least for him.

Biting back a curse, he told himself to let her go. Raine's issues, whatever they entailed, weren't his concern. She was making it clear they didn't have a personal relationship any more. And he had plenty of his own problems to deal with. Like his father, who was almost as stubborn as Raine.

Gingerly, she walked toward the door as if testing the strength in her legs, still looking as if a mild breeze would blow her over.

"Raine," he called, as she crossed the threshold. She glanced at him over her shoulder. "I'm here if you need to talk. Or if you just want someone to listen."

Stark desolation flashed in her eyes, but just as quickly it was gone. "Thanks, but I'm fine. Really. I'll be back in twenty minutes."

This time when she left, he didn't bother trying to stop her.

In Raine's absence, Caleb took control of the patients in their team, including taking on the job of calling the police for the young sexual assault victim.

Their patient care tech, Yvonne, had remained glued to the young woman's side throughout the rape kit exam and even when the police arrived to question her. He didn't complain, even knowing that without Yvonne's help, patients moved slowly through the department.

He kept his distance from Helen Shore, knowing from past experience that most assault patients were far more comfortable with female caregivers. But as he worked, he couldn't get the shattered expression on the young woman's face out of his mind.

Victims of crimes were the most difficult patients to care for. Sexual assaults were right up there next to child abuse, at least in his opinion. Getting angry wasn't exactly helpful to the patients, though, so he schooled his features so that his true disgust and rage toward the assailant didn't show. None of this was the victim's fault.

He could only hope the evidence they obtained would help the police find the bastard who'd hurt her.

When Raine returned, she looked marginally better. Maybe she had finally eaten something. Her face was still lined with exhaustion, though, and he couldn't help wondering why. She looked much worse tonight than she had the night she'd stayed with him in the waiting room. Telling himself that he'd done all he could to open up to her, and that the next move was hers, didn't help. He had little choice but to turn his attention to the matter at hand.

She jumped into the fray without hesitation, quickly picking up on the patient care issues that still needed to be addressed.

"Have we had the drug screen results back yet on Helen Shore?" he asked, when Raine brought him the discharge paperwork on their burn patient.

Her eyes darkened momentarily. "I don't know. I'll check."

He signed the paperwork and then glanced towards Helen's room. The police were still in there, taking her statement. He wasn't sure how much longer they would be, but it didn't really matter since he wasn't about to hurry her out the door.

"Drug screen is positive for flunitrazepam," Raine said, returning to the workstation with a slip of paper in her hand.

Flunitrazepam was the generic name for Rohypnol, the infamous date-rape drug. They wouldn't have the results from the rape kit for several days, but this pretty much sealed poor Helen's fate. There was no doubt in his mind that her rape kit would turn out positive. He sighed and took the results from Raine. "All right. I'll let the patient know."

"I'll go with you." Raine hovered near his elbow as he entered the room. The police officers, one male and one female glanced up at him curiously.

"I have your drug screen results," Caleb said, ignoring the police and focusing on the patient. "Would you rather the officers leave, so I can tell you privately?"

The male police officer looked like he was about to protest, but he needn't have worried, because Helen was already shaking her head.

"No, go ahead," Helen said in a voice barely above a whisper. "They'll need to know either way."

"I'm sorry, but you tested positive for Flunitrazepam, also known as Rohypnol." He handed the drug result to Helen, who barely glanced at it before handing it to the female police officer.

"So there's no mistake," Helen whispered. "He did this on purpose."

"I'm afraid so." Caleb wished there was something he could say or do to make her feel better.

"That's the second case of Rohypnol from the After Dark nightclub in the past few months," the female officer said in disgust. "Could be the same bastard."

Beside him, he heard Raine suck in a harsh breath. And then suddenly she was gone. When he finished in Helen's room, he found her out at the desk working on the computer.

"We have a new admission coming in, new onset abdominal pain," she told him as if nothing was wrong.

"Okay, let me know once you get a set of vitals and a baseline set of labs. Could be his gall-bladder."

"Sure." The forced cheerfulness in her tone bothered him.

But it wasn't until much later, that he realized why. That the shattered look in Helen Shore's eyes reminded him too much of the haunted expression in Raine's.

Raine could barely concentrate as she prepared a summary report for the on-coming shift. Her assault and Helen's may have been by the same person. The idea was staggering. She hoped and prayed the police would find the guy, and soon.

After she finished with report, she gave a small sigh of relief. At last, her interminable shift was over. All she needed to do was to finish up the discharge paperwork on Helen Shore and she could leave.

Taking a deep breath, she entered Helen Shore's room. Yvonne had left the patient's bedside at eleven, since there was currently a hospital ban on over-time. Helen had dressed in her clothes but clutched the blanket around her shoulders, like a lifeline. Raine could relate, and she had no intention of taking it away from her.

"I have your discharge paperwork, Helen." Raine approached her bedside and handed her the slip of paper listing her follow up appointment for the next week. "Do you have any questions before you go?"

Helen slowly shook her head. "No. The other nurse told me she wouldn't have the rest of my test results for a few days. Not that it matters, much," she added bitterly. "I doubt the police will ever find the guy."

"They will." Raine injected confidence in her tone, even though she held the same doubts. She pulled up a chair to sit beside her. "Helen, you need to seek professional help in order to get through this. I know the name of a good therapist, if you don't have one."

"The social worker gave me a list." Helen stared morosely down at her hands. "But what good is talking about it? Doesn't change what happened."

"No, it won't." Raine empathized with the young woman's helpless anger. Especially if it was possible the same guy attacked them both. The After Dark nightclub should be forced to close until this bastard was caught. Even the police didn't believe it was a coincidence. Detective Carol Blanchard had promised to be in touch if she had any evidence, but so far Raine hadn't heard a thing.

She gathered her scattered thoughts. "There are support groups, however. Other young women like yourself, who've been through the same thing." Raine had attended one of the support group meetings, but hadn't found it particularly helpful. She offered the option though, because everyone coped differently.

And she was hardly the expert in coping strategies. She'd thought she was doing so well.

Only to fall completely apart, tonight.

"I'm afraid to go home," Helen admitted in a low voice. "He knows where I live. What if he comes back?"

Raine understood. She'd experienced the exact same fear. In fact, she hoped to move once her lease was up. And she'd been sleeping on the sofa with Spice, unable to face her bed. "Do you have someone to stay with you?"

"I could ask my sister."

Raine gave a nod of encouragement. "I think that's a good idea. And add a deadbolt lock to your door if you don't have one already. Literature shows that date-rape perpetrators don't go back to the same victims, but it doesn't hurt to be extra-careful."

"I will, thanks."

She leaned over and covered the woman's hand with hers. "Remember, Helen, you're not alone. Try the support group, or talking to a therapist. Unfortunately, date rape is more common than the average person realizes."

Helen lifted her head to meet her gaze. "Sounds like you've had some experience with this," she said.

For a moment Raine longed to blurt out the truth. But she was supposed to be the nurse, helping and supporting the patient, not the other way around. The words stuck in her throat. "I—I've cared for other patient's in similar circumstances," she murmured evasively. "And I can imagine what you're going through. Please take care of yourself, okay?"

"Okay."

Raine walked with her outside to the parking lot where she'd left her car. She stared after Helen for a long moment, before turning to head back inside to swipe out. She couldn't wait to get out of there.

Caleb stood behind her and she caught herself just in time to prevent herself from smacking into him.

"Did you need something?" she asked testily. She wasn't in the mood for a confrontation. Not now. She wanted to go home.

"Yeah. Do you have a minute?"

"Not really. I need to go inside to swipe out." She tried to sidestep him, but Caleb didn't take the hint, turning and following her inside to the nearest time clock where she could swipe her ID badge, formally ending her shift.

She suppressed a sigh and faced him. "Caleb, couldn't we do this some other time? I really don't feel well. I've been sick to my stomach. I think I'm catching some flu bug or something."

"Stop it, Raine. I know the truth."

Her jaw dropped and she stared at him. He knew? How was that possible? No one knew. Except her boss, and Theresa had promised not to say a word.

Had she inadvertently said something when she'd passed out?

"You do?"

"Yes." He crossed his arms over his chest and stared at her. "And I'm not letting you go until you agree to talk to me about it."

CHAPTER SEVEN

RAINE stared at him in shock. To hear him blurt out so bluntly that he knew the truth was staggering. "No. I…can't talk about it. I'm sorry." She turned away, heading for the employee parking lot, wanting nothing more than to go home, to recover from her emotionally draining shift.

But once again Caleb followed her outside. She tried to think of something to say to make him go away. But her mind was blank. And one glimpse at the stubborn set of his features told her he wasn't going to let her go easily.

"You shouldn't drive when you're this upset." He took her arm, steering her towards where his car was parked.

For a moment she tensed beneath his touch, wanting to pull away, but then her shoulders slumped with exhaustion. She simply didn't have the energy to fight. Going along with him was easier than arguing. He opened the passenger door of his car and gestured for her to get inside.

She did, without uttering a single protest.

He slid behind the wheel, glancing at her, but not saying anything. The silence should have been oppressive but, oddly enough, she took comfort in his presence. Maybe because taking care of Helen had brought her suppressed fears to the surface.

He pulled out of the parking lot and headed towards his house, without bothering to ask if she was okay with his decision.

She didn't protest. She was secretly glad he hadn't taken her back to her apartment. Her imagination tended to work overtime there.

"How's your father doing?" she asked when he pulled into the driveway.

He glanced at her. "Better. Still in pain, but overall much better."

"I'm glad," she murmured.

After parking the car, he headed up to his house and unlocked the door. She followed him inside, smiling a bit when Grizzly greeted her enthusiastically.

For a moment she buried her face against his silky fur, hanging onto her self-control by a thin thread. She'd been in Caleb's house often while they'd dated. After her emotionally draining shift, the welcome familiarity of Caleb's house soothed her soul.

She'd missed him. Desperately. They'd shared some very good times, before she'd realized the extent of his inability to trust. And then it was too late. She'd made a terrible mistake.

"Grizz likes you," Caleb said, watching her pet the dog as he made a pot of coffee. "He's not that excited when I come home, more like disappointed that I'm not my father."

She didn't know how to respond, worried she'd burst into tears if she tried. Back when things had started to get more intense between them, she'd wondered what it might be like to share Caleb's home with him. She glanced around, liking the way Caleb's kitchen overlooked the living area, the cathedral ceiling providing a spacious feel. She took a seat on the butter-soft deep blue leather sofa. Grizzly followed her, sitting on his haunches in front of her and placing his big head on her lap. His soulful eyes stared up at her adoringly, wordlessly begging for attention. She pressed her face to the silky fur on the top of his head.

The sharp stab of regret pierced deep.

Caleb brought in two mugs of steaming coffee. She could smell the enticing scent of the vanilla creamer she loved. With a guilty start, she realized he must have bought it with her in mind, anticipating a night in the not-too-distant future when she might stay over.

And if things had been different, they might have spent the night together. More than once.

Her stomach churned. The nausea surged up with full force. Desperately, she swallowed hard.

There was no point in wishing for something she couldn't have. Caleb hadn't really trusted her before, there was no way that would change now.

And, really, she couldn't blame him.

He settled into the easy chair across from her, as if he didn't dare risk getting too close. She wrapped her hands around the coffee mug, seeking warmth despite the humid summer evening, wondering why he'd brought her here.

His gaze bored into hers. "Raine, I'm sure you'd feel better if you talked about it."

The hot coffee scalded her tongue. She stared into the

depths of her mug, not wanting to admit he was right. "I doubt it."

"Raine, what can I say to convince you? You stayed with me when my father was having surgery—at least let me help you now. As a friend."

She sighed, knowing he was right but somehow unable to find the words to tell him what had happened. She was afraid, so very afraid of seeing the same flare of disgust in his eyes.

"Did you meet someone else? Is that it? Is that what you're afraid to tell me? What happened? Did he move too fast for you?"

She blinked. Another guy? Was that really what he thought?

"I know you, Raine," he continued, obviously on a roll. "You're a passionate woman, but you're also sweetly innocent. He's a rat bastard for taking advantage of you. I can imagine exactly how it happened. A goodnight kiss went too far, and he pushed you into a level of intimacy you weren't ready for."

Dear God. He didn't know the truth. *He didn't know.*

Her mind whirling, Raine wasn't sure how to respond. Slowly, she shook her head.

"Come on. I know something happened." He set his coffee mug aside, untouched. "That's why you acted so strangely with our sexual assault patient. Because you were close to experiencing the same thing. Isn't that right? Dammit, tell me." The pure agony in his tone hit hard.

"No. You've got it all wrong," she said, sinking further into the sofa cushions, wishing she could close her eyes and disappear.

He let out a harsh laugh. "Yeah, right. That's why you have that haunted expression in your eyes. Don't protect the bastard."

Suddenly she couldn't take the pretence. Couldn't continue acting as if everything was fine when it was anything but. Unfortunately, the scenario he'd described might be closer to the truth than he realized. Except for one important fact.

"I'm not protecting anyone," she said finally. "I don't even know who he is."

"What do you mean?" Caleb frowned in confusion. "How can you not know?"

"Because I was given Rohypnol." She forced the truth out past the lump in her throat. "You were right, Caleb. Is that what you want to hear? You were right not to trust me. I flirted with a stranger and I paid the price."

Caleb stared at her, his eyes full of horror.

She forced herself to finish. "You want to know what happened? I'll tell you. I was sexually assaulted by a man I can't remember."

Raine's confession stabbed him in the chest, ripping away his ability to breathe. He'd known she was holding something back, but this was worse. So much worse than what he'd imagined. His mind could barely comprehend what she was telling him.

Raine had been assaulted. By a stranger.

Appalled, he jumped to his feet, unable to sit still. "My God. I…didn't know. Why didn't you tell me?" he asked in a strangled tone.

She hunched her shoulders and shivered. He wanted

to cross over to her, to put his arms around her and hold her tight, but obviously that was the last thing she'd want.

No wonder he'd seen the same shattered expression in her eyes that had been mirrored in their patient's eyes. He'd suspected some guy had pushed her into something, but he hadn't imagined this. Not that she'd been given Rohypnol and raped. He still could hardly believe it. The confession shimmered in the air between them, forcing him to keep his distance, even though it pained him.

"I couldn't," she whispered. "I haven't told anyone."

She hadn't told anyone? Why in heaven's name not? He paced the length of the great room, jamming his fingers helplessly through his hair. He needed to remain calm when all he wanted was to wrap his hands around the bastard's throat, squeezing until he begged for mercy. He was so angry he could barely see. How on earth had she managed? Especially all alone?

Raine shivered again, the uncontrollable movement capturing his gaze. He swallowed a curse and went into his bedroom. He grabbed the blanket off his bed and carried it into the living room. Wordlessly, he draped it around her slim shoulders, trying not to touch her.

"Thank you," she murmured, pulling the blanket close.

The fury he'd buried threatened to break loose. He didn't know how she could sit there so calmly. He wanted to rant and rave, to throw things. He curled his fingers into fists and he began pacing again, still reeling at the news.

He felt sick, realizing she'd gone through the horror all alone rather than seeking comfort from him. And he understood exactly why.

Because he hadn't believed her when she'd called to apologize after he'd seen her with Jake. And she'd assumed he wouldn't believe her about this as well.

He wanted to smack his head against the wall for being so stupid. For not listening to her when she'd called him the next day. Why had he believed Jake, when he hadn't believed Raine?

Grizz must have realized something was wrong, because the black Lab whined and then abruptly jumped up on the sofa, settling against Raine and placing his large head in her lap. He almost told the dog to get down from the furniture.

But when Raine hugged Grizz close, seemingly grateful for the comfort of the dog's presence, he couldn't bear to yell at Grizz to get down. The dog wasn't a threat to her, not in the way a man might be.

The way he would be? He remembered the way she'd tended to keep distance between them the first few times they'd worked together.

But not afterwards. Not when they'd sat in the waiting room together, waiting for news about his father.

He couldn't stand the thought that she might be afraid of him.

"Raine." He stared at her, hating feeling so helpless. "I don't know what to say."

"You don't have to say anything," she said, her voice muffled by Grizzly's fur. "It's enough that you know the truth."

He clenched his jaw and swung away, so she wouldn't see the simmering anger in his eyes. It wasn't enough to know the truth, not by a long shot. He wouldn't be satisfied until the bastard was caught. Helpless guilt grabbed him by the throat.

If he hadn't let his mistrust get the better of him, maybe he could have handled things differently. He knew now he should have given her the benefit of doubt.

And now it was too late to go back, to fix the mistakes he'd made.

The last thing he wanted right now was to do or say anything that could possibly hurt her. Or scare her.

Control. He needed to maintain control. He couldn't think about how she must have gone into the hospital, seeking help. Being examined. Talking to the police.

No wonder she'd fainted.

His imagination was worse than knowing the truth. How was she coping when he couldn't keep the awful images out of his mind? Another man's hands on her. Forcing her to have sex. Taking what she hadn't freely given.

Ruthlessly, he shoved the horrible images away.

"I'm sorry," he said finally. "I should have been there with you. You shouldn't have had to go through that alone."

She didn't answer. When he glanced back at her he could only see her face, the rest of her body was buried beneath the blanket and Grizz. Her eyes had closed, her mouth had relaxed and her lips were slightly parted in sleep.

Caleb let out a deep breath and collapsed in the chair opposite. He scrubbed his hands over his face.

He tried to tell himself he must not have handled things too badly if Raine was comfortable enough to fall asleep on his living-room sofa. Either that or he'd underestimated the comfort provided by Grizz.

Hell, he'd convince his dad to give her the dog if only she'd smile again.

Smile. Yeah, right. He didn't know how in the world she'd recover from this. How did any woman put something like this behind them?

Broodingly, he watched her sleep, his gaze caressing the curve of her cheek, the silkiness of her hair. He remembered with aching clarity, their last embrace. Their last kiss.

He grimaced and closed his eyes, drowning in the bitter-sweet memories. The sexual chemistry between them had sizzled. During their kisses goodnight, it had taken every ounce of willpower he'd possessed to slow things down. Each night the heat had grown more passionate between them. And he couldn't deny that he'd always been the one to pull back, before either of them had got too carried away.

Even though they'd only dated for two months, he'd suspected he was falling for her. And that had caused him to overreact to everything she'd done. He hadn't been able to find a way to stop himself from constantly questioning her.

His selfish fears had pushed her away at the moment she'd probably needed him most.

He opened his eyes and looked at Raine, mourning the loss. His fault. What had happened to Raine was largely his fault. And now there was no going back.

Whatever feelings she might have had toward him were likely gone. What he hadn't destroyed had likely been demolished by her assailant.

Picking up his mug of coffee, he took a sip, grimacing at the cold temperature. His gaze burned with deep regret as he watched her sleep.

Raine opened her eyes, momentarily confused for a moment about where she was. Grizzly let out a deep sigh beside her. She blinked, realizing she was still on Caleb's sofa, suffocatingly warm as a result of being sandwiched between the blanket and the large dog.

She might be sweltering, but she'd also slept the entire night through without waking up. For the first time since the night of the assault.

She'd felt safe with Caleb. And Grizzly.

Feeling better than she had in a long time, she gingerly sat up, surprised to find Caleb asleep in the easy-chair across from her. So both the man and the dog had watched over her. She winced a bit, realizing that the way Caleb's head lay at such an awkward angle he would probably wake up with a severe crick in his neck.

His eyes shot open, startling her.

She licked suddenly dry lips, smoothing a hand self-consciously over her tangled hair. "Good morning."

"Morning." He straightened in the chair, twisting his head from side to side, stretching the tense muscles. "Are you hungry? We didn't eat anything for dinner last night."

Her stomach rumbled and for the second time in as many minutes she was surprised to discover her nausea was absent and her appetite had returned. "Yes, as a matter of fact, I am. Do you want help?"

Caleb shook his head. "No, I'll throw something together. Omelets okay?"

"Sure." The inane conversation helped keep things in perspective. Caleb had always been a nice guy, of course that hadn't changed. But she couldn't lie to herself. She'd caught the fleeting glimpse of appalled horror in his gaze when she'd finally confessed the truth. Luckily, there was no sign of his aversion now.

She untangled her legs from the blanket. "I'll, uh, need to borrow your bathroom for a minute."

"Help yourself. This will take a few minutes, anyway." Caleb seemed to be giving her distance, letting the dog out as she went past him towards the bathroom.

Ten minutes later, feeling slightly more human after washing up a bit, Raine returned to the kitchen. Caleb had changed his clothes too, looking ruggedly handsome in his casual jeans and T-shirt. He was busy pouring the egg mixture into the pan, and then added ham, cheese and mushrooms.

She smoothed a hand over her badly wrinkled scrubs, feeling awkward as Caleb cooked for her. "Are you sure you don't need help with anything?"

"I'm sure. Why don't you sit down at the table? The coffee should be ready in a minute." After a few minutes he pulled plates out of the cupboard, slid two fluffy omelets onto them and carried them over to the table.

For long moments they ate in silence. When the coffee was ready, he poured them each a mug, laced hers with the vanilla-flavored creamer and brought them to the table.

"Thanks," she said, accepting the cup. "I guess I should apologize for falling asleep on you."

"No, you shouldn't." His tone was tense, but his gaze

was uncertain as he glanced at her. "I'm glad you felt comfortable enough to sleep here."

She glanced away, hating the awkwardness that loomed between them.

"Besides, did you really think Grizz was going to let you leave without a fight?" Caleb asked lightly. "He was in doggy heaven, sleeping on the sofa beside you."

A smile tugged at the corner of her mouth, especially when Grizzly's head perked up at his name. "I didn't mind. He was wonderful company."

Caleb took a sip of his coffee, eyeing her over the rim. "You honestly haven't told anyone else? Not even your brothers?"

Her smile faded. She shook her head. "Especially not my brothers."

Caleb frowned. "Elana?"

"No. She and Brock have been so happy, planning the nursery for the new baby, that I couldn't find a way to tell her." She forced herself to meet his gaze. "I've been too embarrassed. Too ashamed to tell anyone."

"You have nothing to be ashamed of, Raine," he said with a frown.

Too bad she didn't really believe him. "I've been seeing a counselor and talking to her has helped," she said instead.

He nodded encouragingly. "That's good."

She set her fork down, not really in the mood to talk about this any more. "Thanks for breakfast, Caleb, but I really should get going."

Caleb didn't pick up on her hint. "Do the police have any leads on this guy?"

"Not that I know of," she admitted.

"They must have something to go on," he pressed. "Surely you remember some of the men who were there that night."

Her stomach cramped and she put a hand over it, as the nausea returned. Like it always did when she thought about how she'd acted that night at Jamie's bachelorette party, dancing and flirting with the various players and fans of the rugby team who had come in to celebrate their win, buying rounds of drinks for their group.

One of whom could have drugged her. Assaulted her.

Had he fathered a child, too?

CHAPTER EIGHT

"RAINE?" She glanced up when Caleb called her name, staring at him blankly when he leaned forward, his gaze full of concern. "You're awfully pale. Are you all right?"

"Fine," she forced herself to answer, willing the nausea away. Telling Caleb the truth had felt good last night, but now she was beginning to regret giving in. Why did he feel the need to keep talking about what had happened? There was no reason to keep harping on it. She wasn't ready to give him every excruciating detail.

As Helen had said, talking about it didn't change what had happened.

And if he knew everything, he'd realize he might have been right to accuse her of wanting other men. Hadn't she attended the bachelorette party that night, flirting like crazy, in an effort to prove she was over Caleb?

Grizz came over to lick her fingers, as if he could sense her distress, and she stroked his silky ebony fur, trying to summon a smile. "If you don't mind, I'd rather not talk about that night. It's been really hard, but I'm trying to move past what happened to me."

Instantly, Caleb's face paled, his gaze stricken. "I'm sorry. I should have realized…"

His self-recrimination wasn't necessary. Being treated differently was part of the reason she'd chosen not to say anything to anyone. She lifted her chin. "I don't want your pity, Caleb. I've been trying to move forward in my life. To focus on all the positive things I have to be grateful for, rather than dwelling on the negative."

He frowned a little and rubbed the back of his neck. "Pity is not at all what I'm feeling right now. I admire you. I think you're amazing, Raine. Truly."

His sincere, earnest expression eased some of the tension in her stomach. "I'm not. Obviously, taking care of Helen proves I still have a long ways to go. But each day gets a little better. At least, it had been, until last night."

If anything, he paled more. "Because you told me? Telling me made it worse for you?"

"No," she hastened to reassure him. "Because of Helen. I *fainted*, for heaven's sake. I thought I was handling trauma fairly well, even though taking care of Becca had been really hard. We saved Greg Hanson, which helped immensely. I thought I'd gotten over the worst, but then Helen came in and I lost it."

"You handled the stress all far better than anyone could expect." He frowned a little. "I knew you'd taken a temporary position in the minor care area. This was the reason?"

"Yeah. I couldn't take off work for more than a week and still pay my rent, so I asked Theresa, my boss, to put me in Minor Care. Just happened that one of the nurses was out on a medical leave so it was easy to cover her hours."

"I thought you were avoiding me," he admitted.

She lifted her shoulder in a half-shrug. "I was avoiding everyone, not just you."

He stared at her for several long seconds, the last few bites of his meal forgotten. "I feel so damned helpless," he said in a low, agonized tone. "Is there something I can do? Anything?"

She started to shake her head, but then stopped. She looked at Caleb, seated across the table from her, keeping his distance from the moment he'd discovered the truth, as if she were some sort of leper. They didn't have the same relationship they'd once had, but certainly over these past few days they'd re-established their friendship. Hadn't they?

"Actually, I could use a hug." The moment the words were out of her mouth, she wished she could call them back as they made her sound pathetic. Hadn't she just told him she didn't want his pity?

"Really?" The flare of cautious hope in his eyes caught her off guard. He quickly rose to his feet and crossed over to her, holding out his hand in a silent invitation.

Was she crazy? Maybe. Reaching out, she put her hand in his and allowed him to draw her to her feet. And then he slowly, carefully, as if she might break, drew her into his arms.

Enticed by his solid warmth and gentle strength, she wrapped her arms around his waist and buried her face against his chest, breathing deeply, as if she could never get enough of his heady, comforting scent. She'd missed this so much! More than she would have thought possible.

Maybe she'd made a mistake by not telling him. She'd avoided it because she'd known that the person he'd once been attracted to was gone for ever. She'd never be that free-spirited girl again. But she might have misjudged him. Caleb would have stood by her as a friend.

She tightened her grip, silently telling him how much she appreciated this. And when his mouth lightly brushed against the top of her head, she sucked in a quick breath, stunned by a flash of desire.

For a moment she closed her eyes, wishing desperately for the chance to go back, to make a better decision.

His broad hand lightly stroked her back, and she knew his intention was probably to offer comfort, but her skin tingled with awareness. She was tempted to reach up to kiss him. Ironically, she was happy to know she could still feel desire, this deep yearning for physical closeness. That what had happened to her, as awful as it was, hadn't stolen everything.

She still wanted Caleb. The attraction she'd felt for him the moment they'd met was still there.

But would he ever trust her with his whole heart?

She closed her eyes against the prick of tears. No, she didn't think Caleb was really capable of trusting her with his whole heart and soul. And crying wasn't going to change that. Enough of the poor-me syndrome. She had a lot to be thankful for. Negative energy wasn't productive.

Taking a deep breath, she let it out slowly. A tiny part of her wanted to stay in his arms like this for ever, but regretfully she pressed a quick kiss against the fabric of his shirt before loosening her grip on his waist. He immediately let go, and her moment of euphoria deflated when she realized the desire she'd experienced was clearly one-sided.

"Thanks," she murmured, determined not to show him how much she'd been affected by his embrace. "I needed that."

"Any time," he said, in a low husky tone.

Surprised, she glanced up at his dark gray eyes, realizing he sincerely meant it. Was it possible he may still have some desire for her? Even after what had happened? She was afraid to hope. "I...uh, should get going. I'm scheduled to work today."

She sensed he wanted to argue, but in the end he simply nodded. "Okay, give me a few minutes to clean up in here, I don't want to leave everything out with Grizzly around."

"I'll help." She stacked their plates and carried them over to the kitchen sink. And as they worked companionably side by side in the kitchen, she caught a glimpse of the future she might have had with Caleb.

If only she'd swallowed her pride and returned his calls instead of going to the bachelorette party in an effort to forget about him.

"Are you ready to go?" Caleb asked, glancing over at Raine. He wished he could come up with some valid or believable reason to encourage her to stay.

Rather than just the fact that he didn't want her to leave.

Holding her in his arms had been amazing. Humbling. He'd known she'd only wanted comfort from a friend and nothing more, so he'd garnered every ounce of willpower to keep his embrace non-sexual and non-threatening, despite his deeper desire for more.

One step at a time. He was still hurt that Raine hadn't come to him sooner, that she'd chosen to ignore his phone calls rather than to confide in him. But she was here now. Had spent the night on his sofa, with Grizz. Which meant she trusted him at least a little.

Didn't she?

"Sure. I'm ready if you are."

He wasn't ready at all, but he searched the kitchen counter until he found his keys. When he turned back to face Raine, he found she'd dropped to her knees to give Grizz a big hug. The dampness around her eyes wrenched his heart.

He couldn't stand the thought that she'd endured all this alone.

The atmosphere in the car during the ride back to the hospital was quietly subdued. He wanted to offer to give her another hug, but worried about coming on too strong. Logically, he knew it was best to let Raine set the pace for what she wanted or was comfortable with. He could only imagine what she'd gone through.

So he didn't reach for her, even though he desperately wanted to.

"Thanks for the ride," she said softly, when he'd pulled up to her car in the parking lot. "And thanks for letting me borrow Grizzly last night. It's the first night I've slept peacefully since…" Her voice trailed off as she fumbled for the doorhandle.

Oh, man, now he didn't really want her to leave, if

last night was the first night she'd slept well since the assault. But she seemed intent on getting out of the car quickly, so he jumped out and came around to open the door for her, trying to think of a polite way to convince her to stay. "I'm sure Grizz would be thrilled if you'd come spend another night on my sofa."

Her lopsided smile tugged on his heart, but she gave a small shake of her head, declining his offer. "Thanks again." She lifted up on tiptoe and brushed a light kiss on his cheek, surprising him speechless. He wanted badly to crush her close, but kept his arms at his sides so he wouldn't scare her. "Bye, Caleb."

He could barely force the words from his throat. "Bye, Raine. I'll be at work tonight too, so I'll see you later."

He stood, staring after her as she climbed into her car and started the engine. And when she backed out and drove away, it was all he could do not to follow her home.

She'd kissed him. Asked for a hug.

Was he a complete fool for thinking her actions were a sign she was willing to give him another chance?

Raine drove home, feeling better than she had in a long time. The cramping nausea that had plagued her endlessly seemed to have vanished.

Maybe her life was finally getting back on track. Telling Caleb, as difficult as it had been, had helped. At least around him she didn't have to pretend any more.

When she passed a drugstore, her previous doubts resurfaced. Quickly making a U-turn, she headed back to the store to purchase a home pregnancy test. Enough procrastinating.

It was time to know the truth, one way or the other.

Despite her extreme self-consciousness, no one looked at her with blatant curiosity when she purchased a two-in-one home pregnancy kit. The company had been smart enough to provide two tests in one box, providing a back-up in case she did something wrong the first time.

Clutching the bag tightly to her chest, she walked up to her second-story apartment and greeted Spice, who sniffed the remnants of Grizzly's scent on her scrubs with feline disdain.

"Don't worry," she said, scratching the cat behind the ears. "You're still my favorite."

Spice walked away, with her tail high in the air, seemingly looking at her with reproach.

Raine took the pregnancy test with her into the bathroom. She took a shower and then sat down to read the directions on the test kit. The process was easy enough and didn't require that she wait until the morning. Without giving herself a chance to change her mind, she carefully followed the instructions. The brief period of waiting seemed to take three hours instead of three minutes.

Gathering her strength and mentally preparing for the worst, she took a deep breath and went over to look at the test strip.

The words *Not Pregnant* practically jumped out at her. She blinked and leaned closer, looking again to make sure she wasn't simply imagining things.

Not Pregnant.

She wasn't pregnant. Her knees went weak and she

dropped onto the seat of the commode, her mind grappling with the news. This was good. She should be relieved she wasn't pregnant.

So why the strange sense of emptiness underlying the relief?

She'd always hoped to have children one day, but not yet. And not like this. But, still, she couldn't quite push aside the feeling.

She shook off her conflicting thoughts. Now she knew. Whatever was bothering her wasn't a baby. She put a hand over her stomach, which still didn't feel totally normal, but certainly not as upset as it had been earlier. Was it possible she'd tested herself too early? She turned back to pick up the box, reading the instructions again. Sure enough, the company did recommend taking the test again after a week, just to be sure.

Another week? She wasn't sure she could stand to wait that long. Hopefully she'd get her period before then.

She put the pregnancy kit up in the medicine cabinet. She could test herself again, but stress was the likely culprit making her feel sick. The fact that most of her nausea had faded after talking to Caleb only reinforced the possibility.

Her counselor had been right. Keeping everything that had happened to her bottled up inside wasn't healthy.

Caleb had sounded surprised that she hadn't told her three older brothers. She loved her brothers dearly, but they'd been completely against her moving to the big city from their small town of Cedar Bluff. They loved her, but if she told them what happened, she feared they would have gone straight into over-protection mode. They would have insisted on moving her back home and never letting her out of their sight again. And she also knew they might have been tempted to confront every rugby fan themselves—taking the law into their own hands.

She shivered, a cold trail of dread seeping down her spine. No, she couldn't tell them. Not yet.

Not until the police had caught the guy.

Maybe not ever.

For a moment she glanced helplessly around her apartment. Was she crazy to just sit back, waiting for the police to get a lead? Sure, they had Helen's case loosely linked to hers, but that news alone didn't mean they had a suspect. Should she be taking some sort of action? Would seeing a face trigger some latent memory?

She was scheduled to work tonight, unless she could find someone to cover for her. Caleb was scheduled to work, too. A part of her wanted nothing more than to take him up on his offer to spend the night again on his sofa.

But she couldn't lean on him too much. She needed to be strong. And maybe that meant taking action, rather than sitting around, doing nothing.

Caleb went to work early, to visit his dad and in hope of seeing Raine.

He'd been tempted to call her several times that day. Only the memories of how he'd over-reacted before when they'd been dating held him back.

She didn't need him constantly hovering. But doing nothing, and not seeing her at all, was killing him.

When he went up to his father's room on the regular

floor, he was disappointed to find Raine wasn't there. But at least his father looked much better.

"Hi, Dad. How are you?"

"Doc says I'm hanging in there. They made me get up and walk in the hallway." His father grimaced as he rearranged the photographs of the animals at the shelter on his bedside table. Caleb had to admit Raine's simple gift was genius.

"I'm glad to hear that. You need to move around if you want to go home." He glanced at the glossy pictures, realizing how in some ways Raine had known his father better than he had. "Tell me about the animals at the shelter."

That was all the encouragement his father needed. He went into great detail on the dogs he'd recently cared for, ending with a particularly engaging Irish setter. "This is Rusty, he's Raine's favorite."

Raine's favorite? She'd seemed quite taken with Grizz last night. Caleb leaned forward to get a better look. "He's cute."

"The color of his coat matches her hair," his father explained with a smile. "Her apartment doesn't allow dogs, or I know she would have already adopted him."

The idea of Raine longing for the companionship of a dog made his gut tighten. She deserved to have a dog as a pet. Look how quickly she'd bonded with Grizzly. He almost said as much to his father, but then realized that if his dad knew how Raine had spent the night, he'd only have more questions. Questions he didn't have the right to answer.

It was Raine's story to tell, not his. And the fact that

she hadn't told anyone but him was enough for him to keep quiet.

"Seems like you and Raine are pretty close," Caleb said.

His father shrugged. "Not really. We don't talk about our personal lives very much. But, yeah, I enjoy working with her."

"She, uh, hasn't stopped in to visit at all today, has she?" Caleb asked casually.

His father's gaze sharpened. "No. why? Is there something going on between the two of you?"

"Not in the way you're thinking," Caleb said wryly. "We work together in the ED, and I was curious, that's all."

"Hrmph." His father scowled at him. "What's wrong with you, son? Are you blind? Can't you see what a great catch Raine is?"

It was on the tip of Caleb's tongue to remind his father he didn't jump into relationships the way he did, but he bit back the retort. Because, truthfully, he had jumped into a relationship with Raine. Faster than he had with anyone else.

And the moment he'd seen her with Jake he'd assumed the worst.

"I'm not blind," he assured his father dryly. "Raine is beautiful and kind. She's also a great nurse."

His father rolled his eyes. "Now you're going to tell me you're just friends."

"We are. Don't push," he warned, when his father looked as if he might argue. "Besides, I have to go. It's almost time for my shift."

"Go on, then. Save lives." His father waved him off.

Caleb walked toward the door, but then turned back. "Dad?" He waited for his father to meet his gaze. "I love you. Take care of yourself, understand?"

His father looked surprised, but then he nodded. "Thanks, Caleb," he said in a gruff tone. "I will. And I love you, too."

Caleb headed down to the emergency eepartment, glancing around for Raine and frowning when he didn't find her. Had she decided to go back into the minor care area, the small exam rooms that were literally located just outside the main emergency department? After several minutes of looking, he sought help from the charge nurse on duty.

"Which area is Raine Hart working in tonight?" he asked.

"She's not here," the charge nurse informed him. "She called and asked Diane to work for her. Diane is assigned to the trauma bay."

For a moment he could only stare at her in shock, his breath lodged painfully in his chest. Raine wasn't working tonight? Why? Because she was avoiding him? Or because she was too upset?

Dammit, he never should have left her alone.

CHAPTER NINE

CONCENTRATING on patient care helped distract him for a while, but every time there was a lull between patients, his mind would turn to Raine. He tried to call her cellphone on his break, but she didn't answer, which only made things worse. By the time he'd reached the end of his shift, he was crazy with fear and worry.

Caleb went home to take care of Grizz and then paced the kitchen, inwardly debating what to do. He glanced at the clock, realizing it was past eleven-thirty at night, but at the moment he didn't care. He let Grizzly back in and then drove straight over to Raine's apartment complex.

She lived in an eight-unit building, on the second floor, in the upper right hand corner. He frowned when he saw the windows of her apartment were dark.

Because she was sleeping? Or because she wasn't home?

He pulled up to the curb, parked his car and got out. There was a long surface parking lot behind the building, and he ambled back to look for her car.

It wasn't there.

So she wasn't home. The knot in his gut tightened painfully, and the old familiar doubts came flooding to the surface. Where was she? Who was she with? What was she doing?

He knew that Raine wouldn't be with another man, not now. Not so soon after the assault. She'd had to gather her courage to ask him for a hug, for heaven's sake. But the edgy panic plagued him anyway. He thrust his fingers through his hair, wishing he could tune out his wayward thoughts.

He'd avoided serious relationships during medical school, concentrating on his studies. After watching the parade of women come and go in his father's life, he hadn't thought he'd been missing much. Until he'd become a resident and met fellow resident Tabitha Nash.

He remembered all too clearly how betrayed he'd felt when he'd walked into their bedroom to see his naked fiancée in the arms of another man. In their bed.

He'd immediately moved out, and had guarded his heart much more fiercely from that point on. Which was why he'd been so willing to believe the worst about Raine when he'd seen her with Jake.

He walked back to his car, climbed behind the wheel and tried to convince himself to go home. Raine was an adult and if she needed him, she knew how to get in touch with him.

But he couldn't make himself turn the key in the ignition.

When he'd met Raine, he'd told himself to go slow. She was four years younger and more naïve than some of the women he'd dated, probably because she hadn't been used to life in the big city. Regardless, her bubbly enthusiasm for life along with the strong pull of sexual attraction had been difficult to resist.

All too soon he'd found himself falling for her. And when they hadn't been together, he'd constantly questioned where she was and who she was with. Even though he'd known he'd been coming on too strong, he hadn't seemed able to stop.

After he'd realized she hadn't cheated on him with Jake, he'd wanted a second chance. Kept thinking that maybe, after some time had passed, they'd be able to get over their issues. But now he wasn't so sure that was even an option. Even after knowing what had happened, as much as he knew Raine's attack hadn't been her fault, he still didn't like to think about how she'd flirted with a stranger, however innocently. Her laughter had always drawn male attention…

He ground the palms of his hands into his eye sockets. He needed to get a grip. None of this was Raine's fault. None of it! He should go home. Sitting out here in front of Raine's building was making him feel like a stalker. Especially when, for all he knew, Raine could have driven home to see her brothers. Maybe she'd finally decided to tell them what happened.

Go home, Stewart. Stop being an idiot.

Bright headlights approached, momentarily blinding him as he was about to put the car into gear. When the oncoming car slowed and the blinker came on, his pulse kicked up.

Raine. Sure enough, the blue car turning into the parking lot was Raine's. She was home.

Relieved, he shut off the car and climbed out, loping around to the parking lot behind the building.

"Raine?" he called, catching her as she was about to go inside.

She whirled around, putting her hand over her heart. "Caleb?" she said, when she realized who he was. "What are you doing here? You scared me to death."

"I'm sorry." He stood, feeling awkward. "I was worried when you didn't come in for your shift. I wanted to come over to make sure you were okay."

She hitched her purse strap higher on her shoulder. "I'm fine."

He frowned when she realized she was dressed in a sleek pair of black slacks and a bright purple blouse. They weren't suggestive in the least, considering she had the blouse buttoned to her chin, but he couldn't imagine she'd dressed up to go and see her brothers. "Where were you?" the question came out harsher than he'd intended.

She arched a brow and let out a disgusted sigh. "You haven't changed much, have you?"

He'd tried not to sound accusatory. Obviously he hadn't tried hard enough. "I'm sorry, I know what you do in your free time isn't any of my business. I swear I'm only asking because I'm concerned about you."

She stared at him for several long seconds, toying with the strap on her purse. "If you must know, I went to the After Dark nightclub."

He sucked in a harsh breath. "What? Alone? Why for God's sake?"

"Shh," she hissed, glancing around. "You'll wake up

the entire neighborhood. And you can relax, it's not as bad as it sounds. I didn't go inside."

Calming down wasn't an option, but he tried to lower his voice even though his tone was still tense. "What do you mean, you didn't go inside?"

Her expression turned grim. "I'm so tired of feeling like a victim, so I decided to take control. To see if I could help find the guy. I went to the nightclub but stayed in my car, watching the various people coming and going, trying to see if any of the faces jogged my memory. But it didn't work." Her face reflected her disgust. "Unfortunately, I didn't recognize a single soul."

Caleb bit his tongue so hard he tasted blood. He would not yell at Raine. Would not chastise her for going to the night-club alone. Even if she had stayed in her car, there was a chance that the guy who'd assaulted her might recognize her and either try for round two or silence her for ever.

He bit down harder, until pain pierced his anger. Finally, he took a deep breath. Everything was fine. Getting her upset wouldn't help matters. He lowered his voice, trying to reassure her. "Raine, I wish you'd told me. I'd have been happy to go with you."

"You were working, but I'll remember that if I decide to go again, which I sincerely doubt, since the entire attempt was pretty useless." She shook out her keys, choosing one from the ring to unlock the door. "Do you want to come in for a few minutes or not?"

Her half-hearted invitation caught him off guard but there was no way in the world he was going to turn her down. "Ah…sure."

She unlocked the door and held it open so he could follow her inside. He'd only been to her apartment a few times as they'd spent more time at his house while they'd been dating. When she opened the apartment door and flipped on the lights, his gaze landed on the sofa, half-buried beneath a blanket and pillow.

She slept on the couch in her own home? Because the bastard had brought her back here? He stumbled, useless anger radiating down his spine. He blocked off the anger, knowing it wouldn't help.

"Uh, make yourself comfortable," she said, her cheeks flushed as she swept away the bedding to make room on the sofa. "Do you want something to drink?"

Whiskey. Straight up. He tried to smile. "Whatever you're having is fine with me."

Her flush deepened. "I don't have beer or wine or anything. I drink a lot of bottled water these days." Her tone was apologetic.

"Water is fine." A soft mewling sound surprised him and he glanced down. "Is that a cat?"

Raine smiled, the first real smile since she'd come home. "Yes. This is Spice." She bent down to pick up the cat who'd strolled into the room, snuggling the feline for a moment. "I've had her about a month now, since I started volunteering at the shelter. But I have to warn you, I think she's jealous of Grizzly."

He crossed over, trying to be friendly with the calico cat, but she hissed at him, raising her hackles, so he backed off. "My dad mentioned you had a soft spot for Rusty, the Irish setter, at the shelter, but that your lease here didn't allow dogs. I'm glad you were able to get a cat."

Raine put the cat on the floor and shooed her away. "Yes, Rusty is adorable. He was brought in as a stray, severely malnourished." Her blue eyes clouded with anger. "We suspect he was abused by a man, since he's wary of the male workers at the shelter. He bonded with me right away, though, as I happened to be there when he was brought in. He's a wonderful dog. I have to say it took me a while to get him calmed down enough to let your father examine him."

His heart squeezed in his chest. Rusty was abused? No wonder Raine had bonded with the dog. The two had been kindred souls, needing each other. Once again, a feeling of helplessness nearly overwhelmed him. There was really nothing he could do to help her. Nothing.

Except to ignore his own issues to be there for her if she needed him.

"I'm glad he has you, then."

She nodded and went into the small kitchenette to get two bottles of water out of the fridge. She came back into the living room and took a seat on the sofa next to him. He was surprised and glad she'd chosen to sit next to him, rather than taking the chair halfway across the room.

Glancing around the apartment, he was struck once again by the fact that she'd taken to sleeping on the sofa. "Would you consider moving?" he asked, thinking she might be able to put the event behind her more easily if she wasn't here in this apartment with the constant reminders. Plus, if she was open to moving, maybe they could find a place that would allow dogs.

"Not right now. Unfortunately my lease goes through

to the end of the year." She twisted the cap off her water and took a long drink.

He could hear the regret in her tone and wanted to offer to pay off her lease just so she could move out. But the Raine he knew valued her independence. He decided it wouldn't hurt to ask around, see if anyone was interested in moving closer to the hospital and potentially taking over her lease. She couldn't fault him for that, could she?

"How is your father doing?" Raine asked, changing the subject.

"He's fine. I went up to see him before my shift. He misses you and the work at the shelter a lot, I think." Caleb stared at his water bottle for a moment. "I didn't appreciate just how much his volunteer work means to him."

Raine's smile was wistful. "Your father loves animals, but he's also pretty social with the other volunteers. I get the sense being alone is hard for him."

"Yeah. He definitely doesn't want to be alone." He dragged his gaze up to meet hers. "I probably should have explained to you a long time ago about how my mom took off when I was five years old, rather than springing that news on you when my dad was heading off to the cath lab."

"I'm sorry, Caleb. That must have been horrible for you."

He shrugged off her sympathy. "We survived, but my dad started dating again shortly afterwards, bringing home a series of stepmother candidates to meet me."

She winced. "I'm sure that didn't go over very well."

"Maybe it would have been all right if my dad had found someone great, but instead he seemed to make one mistake after another." He downed half his water and set it aside. "My dad went through four marriages and four divorces. Hell, you'd think he'd learn but. no, he keeps finding new women and jumping right back into the next relationship. I've finally convinced him to stop marrying them at least."

"I see," Raine said slowly. She didn't look as if she completely agreed with him. "But, Caleb, surely you realize that your father's mistakes aren't your own."

"I made a similar error in judgment," he said slowly. "Remember I told you that my fiancée cheated on me? We were both residents, working a lot of shifts, often on opposite schedules, but I trusted her. Until I came home early one night to find her in bed with another guy." He tried to soften the bitterness in his tone. "Good thing I found out before I married her."

Her frown deepened. "Not all women cheat, Caleb."

He nodded. "I know. Logically, I know that I can't assume the worst. But my gut doesn't listen to my head."

"So you've been overcompensating ever since," she said softly.

"Yes." He let out a heavy sigh. "I'm sorry I didn't believe you. I tried to call you to apologize but you wouldn't take my calls."

She glanced away. "I know. I wish I had. But we can't go back. Even if we had tried again, I doubt our relationship would have survived. Especially not after what I did."

"Raine, please. Don't say that. You didn't *do* anything. The assault was not your fault." He wished he could reach out and pull her into his arms, but he was afraid of scaring her.

"My counselor says the same thing, but saying that doesn't change how I feel." She finally brought her gaze up to meet his.

"I figured you didn't take my calls because you were still angry with me."

She stared at him for a few seconds. "I was angry with you, Caleb," she said finally. "I went to the bachelorette party in the first place to get over you. But afterwards, you need to understand, the real reason I didn't take your calls was because I'd changed. I'm not the same person I was when you first asked me out. I'll never be that person ever again."

Raine finished her water as a heavy silence fell between them. She wished, more than anything, she could ask Caleb to hold her. Despite how they'd broken off their relationship a month ago, she missed him. Missed being with him. When he'd hugged her that morning, she'd felt normal. The way she'd been before the night that had changed her for ever. As if maybe she really was healing.

"Does the attack still give you nightmares?" he asked in a low voice.

"Not exactly." She picked at the label around her empty bottle and then set it aside. "I don't remember anything from that night. Unfortunately, my imagination keeps trying to fill in the blanks."

Caleb's jaw tightened. "I hope to hell they find the bastard."

"Me too." She tried to think of a way to change the subject. Understanding Caleb's past helped clarify his actions. She could clearly see why he'd questioned her all the time about where she was going and who she was going to be with. But even if she had known all this back then, she didn't think she would have done anything differently. She still would have taken a break from their relationship. She still would have attended the bachelorette party with the rest of the girls.

And the outcome would have been the same.

They'd both made mistakes. Unfortunately, hers were insurmountable.

"Raine, you'll get through this," Caleb said finally, breaking the silence. "Maybe it will take time, but you're strong and I know you'll get through this."

He was completely missing the point. "I know I'll get through it, Caleb. It's already been over a month. I've done a pretty good job so far of moving on with my life. I volunteer at the animal shelter and I've returned to work. I know I'll get through this."

"So where does that leave us?" he asked with a frown.

Her heart tripped in her chest. If only it were that easy to salvage what they'd once had. "What do you want me to say?" she asked helplessly. "I just told you I'm not the same person I was before. I'm not the person you were attracted to. And even if I were, what's changed, Caleb? You didn't trust me before. Didn't believe me when I told you Jake had too much to drink that night. What's changed now?"

"I don't know," he said bluntly, and she had to give him points for being honest. "I can promise to try to work through my trust issues. But you won't know if I have or not unless you give me a second chance."

A second chance? Did she dare? "I'm a different person now," she reminded him.

"Maybe you are, but that doesn't mean I've stopped caring about you."

He cared about her? Her heart squeezed in her chest. Was she crazy to even think of trying to renew a relationship with Caleb? Was she even capable of such a thing? She'd enjoyed being held by him, but that was a long way away from actually dating. And there was a part of her that couldn't believe he'd be able to put aside his trust issues that easily. Would it bother him that she'd been with another man, however involuntarily?

She feared that innate distrust would eventually rip them apart.

Yet she trusted Caleb physically. Being with him felt a little like coming home. "I care about you too, Caleb." She took a deep breath and tried to smile. "If you're serious about wanting a second chance, then I'm willing to try, too."

His eyes widened, as if he hadn't expected her to agree. "Really? I promise I won't rush you. We'll take things slow and easy."

She hesitated, wondering if he was going to have more trouble with this than she was. Caleb's imagination could easily run amuck, just like hers had. "I won't break, Caleb. I was the one who asked you for a hug this morning, remember?"

"I remember."

She set her empty water bottle aside and inched closer. "And you told me I could ask for a hug any time, right?"

His expression turned wary. "Yes. But I don't want

to rush you, Raine. Don't feel like you have to do anything you're not ready for."

"I won't," she assured him, reaching out to take his hand in hers, feeling reassured when his fingers curled protectively around hers. "I'm ready for another hug, Caleb. Would you hold me?"

CHAPTER TEN

"OF COURSE. I aim to please," he said lightly, but there was the slightest hesitation before his strong arms wrapped around her, drawing her close.

Raine sighed and burrowed her face into the hollow of his shoulder. She took a deep breath, filling her senses with his warm, familiar, musky scent.

She closed her eyes against the sting of unexpected tears. This was what she'd wanted ever since leaving his house earlier that morning. This was what she'd been missing.

Caleb lightly stroked a hand down her back, and even though she knew he only meant to soothe her, a flicker of awareness rippled along her nerves. He paused when she trembled, and then slowly repeated the caress. This time she bit back a moan as a wave of desire stabbed deep.

"Are you all right?" Caleb asked, his voice a deep rumble in her ear.

"I'm fine," she whispered, trying to hide how much he was affecting her. "This is nice."

There was another moment of silence and she inwardly winced, knowing nice was the least appropriate word to describe how she was feeling. She'd asked for a hug because she cared about Caleb. But responding to him with awareness and desire only confirmed her feelings for him hadn't lessened during the time they'd spent apart.

But did Caleb feel the same way? Somehow she doubted it. Because deep down she knew that if Caleb had ever really loved her, he would have believed in her.

And despite how he'd asked for a second chance, he was treating her like a victim. Someone to protect. Not a partner. If their relationship had stumbled before, she couldn't imagine how they'd manage to overcome everything that had happened.

Were they crazy to even try? Could they really find a way to overcome their problems?

"I'm glad you're not afraid," Caleb murmured. "It's nice to know you can relax around me."

Relax? With her body shimmering with awareness? Was he kidding? She couldn't help but smile. She lifted her head and met his gaze. "I'm not afraid of being close to you like this."

His gaze locked on hers, and his eyes darkened with the first inkling of desire. She went still, afraid to move. Slowly, ever so slowly, he bent his head until his mouth lightly brushed against hers.

Caleb's kiss was whisper soft and so brief she almost cried out in protest when he pulled away. But then he repeated the caress, gently molding his mouth to hers, giving her plenty of time to push him off.

She didn't.

When his arms tightened around her and he shifted

his position slightly to pull her closer against him, she experienced a secret thrill. He kissed her again and again, but didn't deepen the kiss until she opened her mouth and tasted him.

With a low groan, he invaded her mouth, kissing her deeply, the way she remembered.

But after a few minutes of heaven he pulled away, tucking her head back into the hollow of his shoulder, his chest rising and falling rapidly beneath her ear. "Sorry," he muttered.

Sorry? She frowned. "For what?"

"I promised we'd go slow," he said in a low rough voice full of self-disgust. "A few more minutes of kissing you like that and I would have forgotten my promise."

She frowned. "I'm a woman, not a victim," she said, her tone sharp.

He pressed a chaste kiss to the top of her head. "I know, but there's no rush, Raine. Just holding you in my arms is more than enough for now."

She closed her eyes on a wave of helpless frustration. This wouldn't be enough for her. Maybe Caleb needed more time to grapple with what had happened.

He continued his soft caress, stroking his hand down her back and soon her irritation faded. She snuggled against him, relishing the closeness.

Maybe this was Caleb's way of starting over. Like from the very beginning. And if so, he was right.

There was no rush.

Raine realized she must have fallen asleep because her world tilted as Caleb lifted her off the sofa and carried her into the bedroom. She hadn't been in her bed since that night, but she didn't protest—unwilling to ruin the moment with bad memories.

When he slid in beside her, she relaxed, unable to deny the wide bed was much more comfortable than the cramped sofa, despite their bulky clothes. Using his chest as a pillow, she closed her eyes and tried to relax, regretting more than ever that they hadn't made love during the two months they'd been together. If they had, maybe she'd have that memory to sustain her now.

Hours later, she woke up again when Caleb shifted beneath her. This time she felt the mattress give, and she blinked the sleep from her eyes, watching as he sat on the edge of the bed running his fingers through his tousled hair. Her stomach tightened with anxiety. "Are you leaving?"

He twisted toward her, as if surprised to find her awake. He flashed a crooked smile and leaned over to brush a kiss over her mouth. "I don't want to go, but I almost forgot about Grizz. I let him out after work, but that was hours ago. I need to get home to take care of him."

She'd forgotten about Grizz too, but maybe he was just using the dog as an excuse. Sleeping in Caleb's arms had been wonderful, but suddenly it seemed as if the passionate kiss they'd shared had never happened. She tried to smile. "Too bad you can't bring him over here."

He must have sensed the wistfulness of her voice, because he rolled back toward her, stretching out beside her. "Raine, I wouldn't leave at all if it wasn't for the dog. I promised my dad I'd take care of him. I don't think Grizz has ever been alone all night before."

"I know. I'm sorry. Of course you have to go." She was ashamed of her selfishness. Hadn't they agreed there was no rush? Why was she clinging to him, afraid to let him go? "Thanks for staying, Caleb. I appreciate it more than you know."

"Raine," he murmured on a low groan as he gathered her close. "I don't want to leave. But I have to." He kissed her, deeply, his muscles tense, his need evident.

She drowned in the sensation as he gave her a glimpse of what their renewed relationship might hold. But then, all too soon, he broke away, moving as if to get up out of her bed. "You're making this difficult for me. I really have to go," he said in a gravel-rough tone.

She forced herself to let him go. "Give Grizzly a hug for me, okay?"

He stopped, and then turned back to her, propping his hand beneath his head so he could look down at her. "You could come with me. If you don't have other, more pressing plans, we could spend the day together."

She didn't have any plans, much less pressing ones. And spending the day with Caleb held definite appeal. But she didn't want to sound too pathetically eager. "You're not scheduled to work?"

"No. Are you?"

She shook her head. She wasn't needed at the animal shelter today either. What better way to start over than to spend a Sunday together? "All right, if you're sure."

For an answer, he kissed her again. She couldn't help pulling him close to deepen the kiss. "I'm sure," he said, breaking off from the kiss. "And we'd better leave soon, because I'm very close to not caring if Grizz relieves his bladder in my house."

She laughed, feeling light-hearted for the first time in weeks. She gave him a playful push. "All right, let's go."

Caleb scrubbed the exhaustion from his face as he waited for Raine to finish in the bathroom.

Holding Raine in his arms had been worth sacrificing his sleep. He didn't regret a moment of their night together. Kissing her, holding her, had been a test of his willpower.

Maybe his body was hard and achy this morning, but he didn't care. Somehow he'd managed to ignore his needs and give Raine the security she deserved. Her peace of mind was far more important than his discomfort.

Long into the night, he'd been unable to keep his imagination from dwelling on what she'd been through. He'd only brought her into the bedroom after she'd almost fallen right off the sofa. He'd hoped he could help her get over her aversion to sleeping in her bed.

Unfortunately he'd been tortured by images of how the bastard had brought her here, taking Raine against her will. He was surprised his suppressed anger and tense muscles hadn't woken her up.

Grimly, he told himself that focusing on what had happened wasn't going to help rekindle their relationship. He needed to get over it. And soon.

The way Raine had responded to his kiss proved she was on the road to recovery. He refused to hamper her healing in any way. If she could get past what had happened, surely he could do the same.

"Okay, I'm ready," she said, hurrying back into the

living room where he waited. She poured fresh water into a bowl for Spice and then gave the cat a gentle pat. "See you later, sweetie."

"We could bring Spice if you want. Maybe Grizzly will grow on her," he said, eyeing the cat doubtfully.

Raine brightened, but then reconsidered with a shake of her head. "That's a good idea, but maybe some other time."

He hid his relief. Considering the way the cat had hissed at him, he couldn't imagine Spice would be all too thrilled to meet Grizz, but he'd wanted the decision to be hers.

When they got to his house, he couldn't help feeling guilty when he found Grizz stretched out in front of the door, obviously waiting for him. The dog jumped excitedly, his tail wagging furiously when Raine came in behind him.

"Come on, Grizz, go outside first," he muttered, shooing the dog out back.

The dog took care of business and then came back to the door, looking eager to come back in. Raine opened the door for Grizz as he put out food and water for him.

"I need to call the hospital, see how my dad is doing," Caleb said, glancing at the clock. "And I'd planned to visit today, too, if you don't mind."

"Of course I don't mind," Raine said, looking affronted.

He flipped open his cellphone to call Cardiology. It took a few minutes before he was connected with his father's nurse.

After Caleb explained who he was, the nurse sounded relieved to hear from him. "Your father is not having a good day. He's refusing to get out of bed and has been crabby with the nurses. His surgeon has been in to see him, though, and medically he's doing fine. Emotionally, not so well."

He didn't like the sound of that. "Okay, let him know I'm coming to visit. And tell him I'm bringing company. Hopefully that will cheer him up."

"I will."

He closed his phone and glanced at Raine. "Dad's crabby today, refusing to get up and overall being a pain to the staff. I hope it's not a sign he's taking a turn for the worse."

Raine frowned at the news. "I hope not, too." She glanced down at Grizzly, who'd finished inhaling his food and had come over to nudge her hand with his head, seeking some attention. "Hey, I have an idea. Maybe we can take Grizzly in to visit."

Caleb stared at her. Had she lost her mind? "Since when are dogs allowed to visit patients? Especially on a surgical floor? And I think he's a little too big to sneak in."

"No, really, this could work." Raine took out her own cellphone and dialed a number. He soon realized she was talking to someone in the safety and security department. "Hi, Bryan? This is Raine Hart. How are you? It's nice to talk to you, too. Hey, I'd like to invoke the pet visitation policy. There's a patient, Frank Stewart, on the third-floor cardiac surgery unit who's depressed today. He's a veterinarian, volunteering his time at the animal shelter, and I'd like to schedule a visit with his black Lab, Grizzly."

Caleb listened in astonishment. A pet visitation

policy? He'd never heard of such a thing. But apparently Raine knew all about it and, more, she knew how to arrange the visit.

"Great. We'll be there in two hours, then. Thanks very much." Raine's expression was full of triumph as she snapped her phone shut. "It's all set. We need to stop by Security and the nurses will arrange for your dad to be brought down in a wheelchair to the family center. There's a private conference room we can use."

"Amazing," Caleb murmured. And he wasn't just talking about how she'd picked exactly the right way to cheer up his dad. Raine was a truly amazing woman in all the ways that mattered. "All right. Hopefully this will help to cheer him up." Because if this didn't work, he was afraid nothing would.

Caleb couldn't believe no one stopped them as he and Raine walked into the front door of the hospital, holding Grizzly's leash. Following the rules, they crossed over to the security offices, located down the hall from the main lobby.

"Hi, Bryan," Raine greeted the tall, rather young-looking security guard with a hug. For a moment he wondered if there had once been more between Raine and the handsome officer. A sharp pang of jealousy stabbed him in the region of his heart. "Good to see you. How's Melissa? And the baby?"

"They're great," Bryan said.

Belatedly, Caleb noticed the security officer's wedding ring. Cursing himself for being an idiot, he reached down to pat Grizz. Damn, he'd done it again.

Jumped to a stupid conclusion without giving her the benefit of the doubt.

"I think your patient is already down here, waiting for you." Bryan led the way down toward the family center conference room.

Sure enough, the door of the conference room stood ajar and he could see his father, slumped in a wheelchair with his eyes closed, looking almost as bad as he had that first night in the ICU. Alarmed, he pushed the door open and rushed in. "Dad? Are you all right?"

"Huh?" His father straightened in his seat, prising his eyes open. And then his entire face lit up, brighter than a Christmas tree, when he saw the dog. "Grizzly! Come here, boy."

Caleb let go of the leash, relaxing when his father bent over to pet the dog, who immediately tried to crawl up into his father's lap, not that the ninety-pound dog would fit.

"Grizz, it's so good to see you," his father crooned, lavishing the dog with attention. "Did you miss me? Huh? Do you miss me, boy?"

Caleb was very glad Raine had arranged the visit. When she came up to slip her arm around his waist, leaning lightly against him, he realized why his father kept trying to find someone to share his life with. Because it was nice to share everything, good times and bad, with someone.

He'd only been in kindergarten when his mother had taken off, but he was ashamed to realize he hadn't really looked at the situation from his father's point of view in the years since. His father had been abandoned by his wife. And he'd had a small son to care for while trying to run a veterinary practice. Could he blame his dad for wanting someone to share his daily life with? For wanting help in raising a son?

Was it his father's fault he'd picked the wrong women? His father deserved better. He suddenly he couldn't stand the thought of his father being alone.

"Have you thought about patching things up with Shirley?" he asked abruptly.

"Shirley?" His father's face went blank for a moment, and then the corner of his father's mouth quirked upward. "You mean Sharon?"

Oops. Damn. "Yeah, that's it. Sharon."

Raine scowled. "Wait a minute—Sharon? What about Marlene Fitzgerald? From the shelter?"

"Marlene?" His father's cheeks turned a dull shade of red and suddenly every iota of his father's attention was focused on Grizz. "We're just friends," he muttered.

"Just friends?" Raine's brows hiked upward. "Really? Because she looked devastated when she heard you'd had emergency open heart surgery."

She had? Caleb was exasperated to discover Raine knew more about his father's recent love life than he did.

"She came to visit, but I sent her away." His father frowned. "A woman wants a man who'll take care of her, not an invalid like me."

Caleb hid a wince, because he could certainly understand. Starting a relationship so soon after open heart surgery probably wasn't a good plan.

"That's not true," Raine protested, going over to kneel beside his father's wheelchair. Grizz licked her cheek, but she didn't take her imploring gaze off his father. "A woman wants a man to be her partner. And the whole point of a partnership is taking turns helping each other."

Caleb stared at her as the full impact of her words slowly sank into his brain.

He'd been an idiot. Like his father, Raine didn't want to be an invalid. She'd said as much, hadn't she? She didn't want him to take care of her, the way he'd been trying to do since he'd discovered she'd been assaulted.

His gut clenched in warning. He'd asked for a second chance, but he knew that a big part of his reasoning had been because he'd wanted to help Raine through her ordeal. To support her.

But obviously that wasn't at all what she wanted from him.

CHAPTER ELEVEN

A COLD chill trickled down his spine. Could he be a true partner for Raine? Could he put aside his doubts for good? God knew, he wanted to.

Just minutes earlier he'd watched her hug Bryan, the young security guard, and instantly the old familiar doubts had crept in.

He wanted a second chance with her—but if he blew it this time, he knew there wouldn't be another.

"Maybe you're right," his father said, giving Raine a half hopeful, half uncertain look. "But I can barely get around. I'll wait to talk to Marlene until after I get back on my feet."

"I think you should talk to her sooner rather than later," Raine mildly disagreed, scratching Grizzly behind the ears. "Unless you think for some reason she won't get along with Grizz?"

"The dogs at the shelter seem to like her well enough, and she's not afraid of them. I'm sure Grizz will like her, too."

"Well, that's good, because you certainly wouldn't

want to call on a woman who doesn't get along with your dog," Raine lightly teased.

"Sharon was afraid of Grizz," his father said. "I should have known that was a bad sign. I think Grizz could tell, too because he growled at her. And he never growls at anyone."

Raine laughed, a light-hearted sound that reminded Caleb of the wonderful times they'd spent together. She'd told him she wasn't the same woman she'd been before, but he didn't agree. The old Raine was still there, and given enough time and healing she'd return. "Definitely not a good sign. Spice hissed at Caleb, too," she confided.

He put a lid on his troublesome thoughts. "Guess that means I don't have much of a chance, huh?" he asked in a light tone.

Raine glanced over her shoulder at him and raised a brow. "I don't know. I'll think about it."

His father glanced between them with a knowing smile, looking a hundred times better than when they'd first arrived. "What plans do the two of you have for today?"

"Nothing special," Raine said with a shrug.

"Why not go to the state fair?" his father persisted. "It opened on Friday and goes all week."

"The fair? I haven't been on the Ferris wheel in ages," Raine murmured. But her eyes brightened with interest, and Caleb knew his father had presented the perfect solution.

"I haven't been to the fair lately either, but I'm up for it if you are," he said, hoping she'd agree.

Her smile widened. "I'd love to."

"Have fun," his father said, shifting in his seat. He glanced longingly at the dog. "Do you think the nurses would notice if Grizz stayed with me in my room?"

"I think they might become a tad suspicious, especially when he needs to go outside," he said wryly. "How much longer will you need to stay in the hospital?"

"They're talking about sending me home in a day or two, depending on how well I can walk," his father admitted.

"Well, I guess you'd better get walking, then." He made a mental note to talk to Steven Summers for himself. "I'll be happy to move in for a while to help once you're home."

"Thanks." The older man leaned over to give the dog one last hug. "See you soon, Grizzly," he murmured.

Caleb felt bad leaving his father at the hospital, but they needed to take Grizzly home. "Good idea, bringing Grizz in for a visit," he said to Raine as they walked with Grizzly outside.

"He really perked up, didn't he? And I bet Marlene would be willing to help your father, too, if he'd only give her a chance."

"Maybe he will." Caleb didn't want his father to be alone, but he also didn't want his father to rush into anything.

He wanted his father to take his time, to find the right woman to partner with.

And as he glanced at Raine he knew it was time to take his own advice. Raine wasn't Tabitha. She was a hundred times better than Tabitha. If he couldn't trust Raine, he couldn't trust anyone.

* * *

Thrilled with the idea of going to the state fair, Raine could hardly maintain her patience as Caleb took care of Grizz. She hadn't been to the fair since going with her older brothers, years ago.

When Caleb was finally ready to go, she nearly skipped with anticipation. The sounds and scents of the fair reminded her of happier times.

"There's the Ferris wheel," she said, clutching Caleb's arm with excitement.

"Do you want something to eat first? Or after the ride?" he asked.

"Eat first, but I don't want any of that weird fried food on a stick," she said, grimacing at the people in front of them who were eating deep-fried Oreo cookies on a stick. "I'm sorry, but that looks disgusting."

"Okay, nothing on a stick," he agreed good-naturedly.

They settled on burgers, and then wandered down the midway. She remembered the Ferris wheel as being huge, but now that she was an adult the ride wasn't nearly as impressive.

But Caleb had already bought their tickets, so she stood in line beside him. When it was their turn, she felt like a giddy teenager, sliding into the seat next to him.

Caleb put his arm around her and she leaned against him contentedly as they began their slow ascent. When they reached the top, she gazed down at the fairgrounds, amazed at how far she could see.

"Look at all the people," she said in a low whisper, suddenly struck by how much more crowded every-thing looked from up here.

"Check out the lines of people streaming in through the entrances," Caleb pointed out. "We must have arrived well before the rush."

She leaned a little closer to Caleb, abruptly glad to be up in the Ferris wheel, far away from the crowd. She'd never been enochlophobic before, but she was feeling apprehensive about going back down amidst the masses of people.

"You're not afraid of heights, are you?" Caleb asked, as if sensing her fear.

"No, not at all." And she wasn't afraid of crowds either. She was determined not to let anything ruin her day.

"Good." He leaned down and pressed a soft kiss against her mouth.

The ride was over too soon. When their car came to the bottom of the Ferris wheel and stopped, she stepped off with reluctance.

She led the way back down the midway, but people were pressing against her, and she must have muttered "Excuse me" a dozen times in her attempt to get past.

When a particularly large man shoved her backward, a rush of panic exploded. "*Let me through!*"

"Raine?" She could hear Caleb calling her name, but couldn't see him. And suddenly she wasn't standing in the midway of the state fairgrounds any more.

The music of the After Dark nightclub was deafening. Her feet ached from dancing, but suddenly she just wanted to go home. But where was Jamie? And the rest of her friends?

Sandwiched between two guys, she tried to brush

past, but their large frames held her captive. Yet despite the close contact, she wasn't alarmed.

"Hey, you're not leaving already, are you?" the one guy asked, taking hold of her arm. "I thought we were celebrating? I just bought you a drink."

She'd recognized two of the rugby followers they'd danced with earlier. The one guy talked a lot, but the other one just looked at her. "Just a soft drink, right?" she'd clarified, before accepting the glass.

"Yeah, just a soft drink."

The brief memory faded away. That had been the last thing she remembered before waking up the next day, feeling extremely hungover. Her body had ached in places it shouldn't have but it hadn't been until she'd found the white stain on her sheets that the sick realization had dawned.

She'd been drugged and raped.

"Raine!" Caleb's worried face filled her field of vision, his hands lightly clutching her shoulders. "What happened? Are you all right?"

She tried to nod but realized her face was wet with tears so she shook her head. "I need to get out of here," she whispered. "Can we leave now? Please?"

Caleb's expression turned grim and he nodded, tucking her close. "Excuse us," he said loudly, using his arm as a battering ram as he barreled through the crowd. "Move aside, please."

It seemed like an eternity but they eventually broke free of the worst of the mass of people. "What happened?" he asked in a low, urgent tone. "Did you see someone who looked familiar?"

She shook her head, unable to speak. He worried that she'd seen someone from that night, and she had, but only in her repressed memories. Caleb must have understood, because he didn't push for anything more but simply tucked her under his arm and led the way out of the fairgrounds to the street where they'd parked their car.

Safe in the passenger seat, she slowly relaxed. "Thanks," she murmured.

His gaze was full of concern. "I'm sorry. I didn't realize the crowds would get to you."

"Neither did I," she admitted. "And it wasn't just the crowd, it was being in that crush that brought back memories of that night."

Caleb started the car and pulled into traffic. "Do you think you could recognize him?" Caleb asked.

"Maybe." But she wasn't completely certain. For one thing, there had been two guys and she was sure only one of them had taken her home. But which one she had no idea. They'd claimed to be friends of one of the rugby players, but which player? "The nightclub was really crowded, and it was hard to move, just like it was on the midway. Two guys bought me a soda, but unfortunately, that's the last thing I remember."

"It's okay. They'll catch him," Caleb said with a confidence she was far from feeling. When he reached out to take her hand, she grasped it gratefully. She was relieved when he let the topic go without pressing for more details.

"Sorry we didn't get to see much of the fair," she said, feeling slightly foolish now that the initial panic had faded.

"It doesn't matter, Raine. I was only interested in

spending the day with you." His sincere tone made her believe he truly didn't mind. "I'm sure Grizz is lonely. I'll cook you dinner at my place instead."

"Really?" she couldn't remember him ever offering to cook for her when they'd dated before. She had to admit she was impressed with his willingness to start over. "Are you sure you don't mind?"

"Of course I don't mind. We'll have to stop at the grocery store, though, to pick up a few things."

"Okay." When they stopped at the grocery store, located not far from Caleb's house, they bought more than just a *few things*. Caleb started with thick ribeye steaks and fresh mixings for a salad, but somehow their entire cart was soon full of other goodies before they made their way to the checkout.

She'd never grocery shopped with a man before, other than with her brothers, but in her experience with the men in her family she knew the food they'd purchased today would be lucky to last a half a week. Less, if she stayed with him.

Not that he'd invited her to stay, she reminded herself. This was their second chance, and there was no rush.

Pushing the longing aside, she focused on spending the rest of the day with Caleb, without being affected by the shadows of the past.

Caleb tried to remain nonchalant after Raine's meltdown at the state fair, but he couldn't help sending her worried glances when she wasn't looking.

The frank fear etched on her face would remain seared into his memory for a long time.

He was stunned she'd remembered something from the attack. He'd wanted to press for more information about that night, but had forced himself to back off, grimly realizing the details he'd wanted to hear would only hurt her.

And he didn't want to hurt Raine, ever again.

He watched her play fetch with Grizzly out in the back yard; the dog had been ecstatic to see them when they'd returned home. Being with Raine seemed so right. As if she belonged here. Although in his scenario she'd be playing with her own dog, Rusty, instead of Grizz. Not that he wouldn't have minded keeping Grizz either. But clearly his dad needed Grizzly more than he did.

As he put the groceries away, he wondered how to broach the subject of her staying here with him overnight. The thought of letting her go home to face the night alone made him feel sick to his stomach. No matter how he tried, he couldn't get over feeling protective of her.

But he'd do his best to be a partner, like she wanted.

He made a quick call to his father's surgeon, verifying that indeed his father would likely be discharged on either Monday or Tuesday. He then made arrangements to be off work for a few days so that he'd have time to help his father make the transition home.

After that, he made two salads, cutting up the ingredients and putting everything in the fridge for later. He went outside, to find that Raine had dropped into one of his wide-backed Adirondack chairs, exhausted after her romp with Grizzly.

"Let me know when you're hungry, and I'll throw the steaks on the grill," he said, taking a seat in the chair next to hers.

"I'm ready whenever. I'm glad we came back, I think poor Grizz has been lonely."

"Yeah, I'm sure he'll be much happier when my father is finally discharged from the hospital." He reached over to scratch Grizz behind the ears. "I talked to Dr. Summers and he told me to plan on my father coming home tomorrow or Tuesday."

"That's wonderful news. I'm sure it will take a while, but your father will feel much better now that he's had the surgery."

"I hope so." He stood and walked over to light the charcoal sitting in the bottom of the grill. "Guess dad won't be eating steaks for a while," he mused.

She let out a quick laugh. "Nope, guess not. Good thing we're having them tonight, then, isn't it?"

He tried to make sure the atmosphere between them stayed relaxed and companionable as he grilled the steaks, sautéing some fresh mushrooms on the side. He brought out the salads and two TV trays so they could eat outside. He thought about offering to open a bottle of Merlot but, remembering Raine's preference for water, decided against it.

Certainly he didn't need any alcohol. Raine's presence was intoxicating enough.

As dusk began to fall, the mosquitoes came out, so reluctantly they carried everything inside.

Together, they cleaned up the mess Caleb had left in the kitchen. Working as a team, the chore didn't take long.

"Caleb, do you mind if I ask you a question?" Raine asked, after they'd finished.

"Of course not." He draped the damp dishtowel over the counter to dry.

"Do you want me? Intimately? The way you did before?" she asked, her cheeks stained bright red. "Or are you turned off because I was raped?"

What? He wanted to kick himself for making her doubt his feelings. Instantly he crossed over to her, clasping her shoulders and trying to encourage her to meet his gaze. "No, Raine, I'm not turned off by what happened. Why would you think that?"

"Because each time you kissed me last night, you were the one to pull away."

He couldn't deny it. But when he'd pulled back, it had been because he'd been close to forgetting what she'd been through. "Only because I promised I wouldn't rush you into doing anything you weren't ready for."

She bit her lower lip. "And what if I can't know what I'm ready for if we don't try?"

He stared at her. Was she really saying what he thought she was saying? "Raine, just a few hours ago you freaked out at the fair. I think that shows you still have a way to go before fully recovering from the assault." And he'd never forgive himself if he frightened her.

She must have read his mind. "You won't frighten me, Caleb. I freaked out at the fair because of the strangers surrounding me. But I didn't feel the least bit frightened last night. In fact, I felt safe and normal for the first time in weeks. You helped me realize that I've gotten over the worst of what happened." She frowned. "But I know that just because I'm getting over what happened, it doesn't mean you have."

Her insight struck a chord, because she was right. How long had he known about her assault? Three days? Not nearly enough time to come to grips with what she'd been through. But that was his problem to wrestle with, not hers. And he did want her, too much for his peace of mind. "Raine, please don't worry about me."

"I won't worry about you if you agree to stop worrying about me. Deal?"

"Deal," he said, his voice clogging in his throat when she stepped closer, wrapping her arms around his waist.

"Kiss me," she whispered.

He couldn't have denied her request to save his soul. He kissed her, lightly at first, but when she responded by melting against him, he deepened the kiss, sweeping his tongue into her mouth.

Last night he'd made the mistake of treating Raine like a victim, and he vowed not to make that same mistake again. He loosened his iron-clad grip on his control, showing her how much he wanted her.

Grizz barked, interrupting their kiss. Caleb struggled to calm his racing heart as he glared at the dog. "What is your problem? Get your own girl."

The dog looked at him, perplexed. Raine giggled. "Maybe he needs to go outside."

Muttering something not very complimentary about the dog, he peeled himself away from Raine long enough to let the dog out. Grizz did his business and then bounded back inside.

He turned back toward Raine. "I'd like you to stay with me tonight. No pressure, we can just sleep if that's all you want."

She tilted her head, regarding him solemnly. "And what if I want more than just to sleep?"

His groin tightened, betraying the depth of his need. Forgetting what she'd been through was easier if he concentrated on her. "Your decision, Raine. Always your decision. We can stop any time."

"Then I decide yes." Her simple words stole his breath. Her faith in him was humbling.

He was damned if he'd let her down.

He barely remembered leading her to his bedroom. One moment they were standing in the kitchen, the next she was in his arms, kissing him like she'd never stop.

He'd planned to take this slowly, to give her plenty of time to change her mind, but when she tugged at his clothes, he could barely suppress a low groan.

Taking control of the situation the best he could, he shucked off his jeans and shirt, keeping his boxers on, and then helped her strip down to her bra and panties. From there he lifted her up and set her gently on the bed.

She gazed up at him as he stretched out beside her. "Slow and easy, Raine," he murmured. "There's no rush, remember?"

"I want you, Caleb," she whispered, stroking her hand down his chest, dangerously close to the waistband of his boxers.

He swallowed hard, and bent to press a trail of kisses down the side of her neck to the enticing V between her breasts, as he stroked his hand down over the curve of her belly, and then lower to the moist juncture of her thighs. "I want you, too. Let me show you how much."

She gasped and arched when he pressed against her mound. "Make love to me," she begged.

"Absolutely," he promised huskily, determined to make this experience a night she'd never forget.

One that would forever replace the dark shadows of the past.

CHAPTER TWELVE

RAINE clung to Caleb's shoulders, her senses reeling from his sweetly arousing touch. They weren't even naked and her body hummed with tension. She knew Caleb was going slow, worried about scaring her—but right now nothing existed but this moment. The two of them together, at last.

His caresses grew more intimate, sending shivers of pleasure rippling down her back. He peeled away her bra and underwear. She lightly raked her nails down his back and the way his muscles tensed and the low groan that rumbled in his throat gave her a secret thrill of satisfaction.

Caleb wanted her. Truly wanted her. And knowing he wanted her was the best aphrodisiac in the world.

When he continued to caress her, driving her to the edge, she sensed what he intended and pulled away. "No, Caleb. Not just me. Both of us together."

He stared at her, his eyes glittering with desire. "Are you sure?"

"Yes, I'm sure." She reached out to stroke his hard length beneath his boxers and he let out a low groan. "You're overdressed," she chided.

He drew back and fumbled for a condom. After stripping off his boxers, he sheathed himself and then rose above her. For a split second she froze, but then he kissed her and she relaxed, knowing this was exactly what she wanted.

As if sensing her moment of unease, he flipped onto his back, tugging her over so that she straddled him. His smoky gray eyes were nearly black with need. "Your choice, Raine," he huskily reminded her.

She stroked his chest and lifted up, until he was right where she wanted him to be. And when she gingerly pressed against him, he let out another low groan.

Beads of sweat popped out on his forehead but he didn't move, refusing to take control. She wasn't very experienced, had only one lover in college, but she lifted her hips and slid down, until he filled her. Even then he didn't move so she repeated the movement, lifting up and down, finding the rhythm and enjoying being the one in control.

He grasped her hips, deepening his thrusts, and she gave a murmur of encouragement. The tension built to the point where she didn't think she could hold back another moment.

And then abruptly, she peaked, spasming with pleasure so intense she cried out at the same moment she felt Caleb pulsating inside her.

Together, at last.

She was asleep when Grizzly nudged her hand. She opened one eye and peered at the clock, noting the sun had just barely begun to peek over the horizon. It was early. Too early. She closed her eyes, trying to ignore him.

Grizz nudged her again, insistently, and she let out a tired sigh, knowing the poor dog probably needed to go outside. Carefully, so as not to wake Caleb, who was sprawled across the center of the bed, she slid out from beneath his arm. Grabbing her jeans and one of his sweatshirts, she hastily dressed before tiptoeing from his bedroom.

She softly closed the door behind her, so he could sleep a little longer, and then met Grizzly at the back door, where he waited rather impatiently.

"Go on, you big oaf," she said fondly, opening the door.

She made herself a pot of coffee, figuring Caleb wouldn't mind. When the coffee finished brewing, she added her favorite vanilla-flavored creamer, and then carried the mug outside.

Curled up in Caleb's Adirondack chair, she watched Grizz sniff the grass and basked in the glorious night they'd shared.

Being intimate with Caleb had been amazing. He had been tender and kind, treating her as a precious treasure yet making it clear how much he wanted her.

Maybe they could make this work. Surely he'd trust her now.

She sipped her coffee and forced herself to face the truth.

She was falling in love with Caleb.

Love. There was a part of her that was amazed, considering everything she'd been through, at how she could actually fall in love with Caleb. Somehow it was easier now to relinquish her heart.

Yet on the heels of her happiness came a warning

chill. What if Caleb didn't feel the same way? Sure, he cared about her, he'd told her that much, but love? In order to love someone you had to trust them completely. Implicitly.

Was Caleb capable of loving her the way she loved him?

Curling her fingers around the steaming mug, she tried to suppress her dire thoughts. He'd promised to work on his trust issues. She wasn't foolish enough to believe it would happen overnight. As long as he was making the effort, she could be patient.

Grizzly sniffed his way around the yard, happily marking every bush and tree with his scent, making her smile. From the very beginning she'd always felt at home with Caleb. There'd been this sense of rightness in being with him.

"Raine?" he bellowed so loudly she started, sloshing coffee onto the front of his sweatshirt. She uncurled herself from the chair, even as Grizzly bounded toward the door.

"I'm out here," she called.

He threw open the door, his gaze landing on her with something akin to wary disbelief. "I couldn't find you."

"Grizzly needed to go out and I didn't want to wake you." She tried to make light of the situation, but his brief yet very real panic couldn't be ignored.

He'd thought she'd left. Like his mother had abandoned him all those years ago. No wonder he found it so difficult to trust.

And in that moment she realized he'd never really

gotten over that feeling of being abandoned. Not really. And though she believed he'd try, she honestly didn't know if he ever would.

Raine began the process of cooking eggs and bacon for breakfast, sensing Caleb was annoyed with himself.

Determined to remain positive, she chatted as if nothing had happened. Caleb needed time and there was no rush. So she put forth her best effort, telling Caleb about some of the other animals at the shelter.

"Which reminds me, I probably need to get home soon," she said lightly. "Spice is going to be very unhappy with me."

"No, Spice is going to be unhappy with me," Caleb corrected. "Especially when you go home smelling like Grizz."

She shrugged. "I love my cat, but someday Spice is going to have to learn to co-exist with a dog, because I really want a dog of my own, too."

Caleb's smile was fleeting, but then he stared broodingly at his plate. "I hope you're not leaving because I acted like an idiot," he said finally.

"No, but tell me, how did you think I'd gotten home without a car? The distance between your place and mine is a pretty long walk."

He shrugged, his expression tense. "I wasn't thinking, it was a knee-jerk reaction."

Like the night he'd come in and found a semi-intoxicated Jake draped all over her, trying to kiss her.

She pushed her plate away. "Caleb, I could tell you I'd never betray you like that, but I'm pretty sure that nothing I can say will convince you. This is something you have to figure out on your own."

He gave a terse nod and rose to his feet. He stacked their dirty plates and then carried them into the kitchen. "I want to change, so maybe I'll take lessons from you."

"Not me," she protested. Her cellphone chirped and she frowned, pulling the instrument from the pocket of her jeans. She recognized her youngest brother's number on the screen. "Hello?"

"Raine?" Michael's familiar voice boomed in her ear. "Is that you?"

"Mikey! It's good to hear from you," she said, sincerely pleased to hear from the youngest of her three brothers. "What's up?"

"Where are you?" he demanded. "I'm at your apartment, and your car is here, but you're not answering the door."

Oh, boy. Her eyes widened in alarm. He was at her apartment? What on earth for? She ignored his overprotective tone. "Yes, Mikey, you're right. I'm not there. I can be there in a few minutes—though, if you need me. Is something wrong?"

"Nothing's wrong, but I'm in town for two days of training and figured I could bunk with my baby sister. I left you a message on your answering machine—didn't you get it?"

He had? She hadn't listened to her messages lately. "Er, no, I didn't."

"So I came to your apartment, and found your car was here, but you're not. You told me you worked second shift, right? I figured I needed to get here before you headed off to work."

She sighed and glanced at Caleb, who was listening to her one-sided conversation with a frown. "I don't work today, and it's fine if you want to stay with me for a few days."

"Where are you?" he demanded.

She refused to respond to her brother's Neanderthal tactics. "I'll be home in about fifteen to twenty minutes. You can either wait for me or go find something to do for a while."

"I'll wait," he said, and she could just imagine the scowl on her handsome brother's face.

"Fine. See you in a bit." She snapped her phone shut.

"Let me guess, one of your brothers?" Caleb asked wryly.

"Yes." She supposed it was a good sign that he didn't assume it was some former boyfriend. "He's at my apartment, waiting for me."

"Then I guess we'd better get going." Caleb let Grizzly outside and then led the way out to his car. "Are you going to tell him?"

"About us? I think he's going to figure it out when you bring me home," she said with a weary sigh. She wasn't in the mood for her brother's macho protectiveness, she really wasn't.

"No, not about us. About the assault."

She couldn't temper the flash of annoyance. "No. Why would I do that?"

"Because he's family, and he obviously cares about you. He should know," Caleb persisted.

After they'd spent the night making love, he went right back to the assault? Disappointment stabbed deep. Hadn't they moved beyond that? "No, he doesn't need to know. And if I were you, I'd worry about yourself, because Michael is not going to be pleased to meet you." At the moment she wasn't so pleased with Caleb either.

He sent her an exasperated glance. "It'll be fine."

"If you say so," she muttered darkly, crossing her arms over her chest.

When Caleb pulled up in front of her eight-unit apartment building, she saw her brother pacing on the sidewalk, talking and gesturing wildly into his phone. Great. No doubt he was telling Ian and Slade all about her spending the night with a man.

Good grief, she didn't need this.

She pasted a smile on her face when she climbed out of Caleb's car. Caleb came round to stand beside her and when Michael saw them, he abruptly ended his conversation and came striding toward her. "Hi, Raine. Who's this?"

"Caleb, this is my brother, Michael. Mikey, this is my friend Caleb Stewart. He's one of the ED physicians on staff at Trinity Medical Center."

"So what? Am I supposed to be impressed he's some sort of doctor?" Michael demanded, glaring at Caleb. "After he's spent the night sleeping with my baby sister?"

She rolled her eyes. "Knock it off. I'm twenty-six years old and you're acting like an idiot. What I do with my personal time is none of your business."

Her brother's gaze narrowed in warning. She'd known he'd react like this, as if she were some sixteen-year-old who couldn't make her own decisions.

"Michael, it's nice to meet you." Caleb stepped forward to offer his hand and she had to give him credit for trying to make peace. Her brother reluctantly shook it. "Raine talks about her three older brothers all the time. I know she cares about you very much."

Her brother's gaze softened a little. "I'm glad to hear that, because you need to know that if you hurt her, the three of us will hold you responsible."

She quickly interrupted to prevent the conversation from going anywhere close to the assault. "I can take care of myself, Mikey. And even if I can't, the mistakes I make are my own. Now, play nice with Caleb, or I won't introduce you to my boyfriends ever again."

"Sure, no problem." Michael rocked back on his heels and gave her a cheeky grin. "But just so you know, I already spilled the beans to Ian and Slade."

She knew it! She scowled at him. "Great. Thanks a lot. I should make you sleep in a hotel." She turned toward Caleb. "See what I mean? I tried to explain what it was like living with them, but you thought I was exaggerating."

The corner of Caleb's mouth quirked upward. "Nah, I knew you weren't exaggerating. I don't have a sister, but if I did, I think I'd probably feel the same way they do." He lifted one shoulder in an apologetic shrug.

"That's right, you would." Michael clapped him on the back, as they finally saw eye to eye on something.

She suppressed another sigh. "Well, grab your gear, then, and come on up. What time does your training start?"

"Noon." Michael glanced at Caleb in surprise when he fell into step beside them. "I hope you don't mind if I bunk here for the next two nights," he said, as if realizing three was, indeed, a crowd. "I haven't seen you in a while and figured this would be a good chance to catch up."

Which was his way of telling her that she'd better not plan on having Caleb stay over while he was there. As if she would.

"It's fine," she assured him. "Caleb's dad is actually scheduled to come home from the hospital either later today or tomorrow anyway."

"The hospital?" Michael's eyebrows rose. "I'm sorry to hear that. I hope he's okay?"

"He had triple bypass surgery and a valve replacement a few days ago, but he's doing much better," Caleb told him.

"I'm glad," Michael said.

"Mikey's a volunteer firefighter and a paramedic back home in Cedar Bluff," she explained for Caleb's benefit.

"I'm impressed. Fighting fires is a tough job."

"Well, I do more paramedic work than anything else," her brother said modestly. "Thankfully there aren't a lot of fires in Cedar Bluff. We have to do a lot more training, though, since we don't get as many chances to work in real fire situations. Which is why I'm here in Milwaukee."

Raine led the way inside her apartment, greeting Spice who lightly ran over to meet the newcomers. Spice veered away from Caleb, but meowed softly and brushed up against Michael's leg.

"She's a cutie. Probably smells Leo, the male tomcat we have down at the station," Michael said, bending down to stroke the cat. "Leo is quite the Romeo."

"Just like you, huh?" Raine said dryly. For all his protectiveness of her, her youngest brother was legendary with women. "Does anyone want coffee?" she called out, heading into the kitchen.

"I do," her brother announced. "Give me a minute to borrow your bathroom."

When her brother disappeared behind the bathroom door, she glanced at Caleb. "Are you all right?" she asked, considering he hadn't said much since meeting her brother.

He threw her an exasperated look. "Raine, your brother doesn't scare me. None of your brothers scare me. Don't worry about it. Although I do see what you mean about what it must have been like living with them. They don't recognize any personal boundaries, do they?"

"Not really." She filled the coffee-maker with water and started the pot brewing. "My parents died when I was just a sophomore in high school. The three of them were really pretty wonderful, moving back home to raise me."

Caleb's gaze was full of sympathy. "That must have been hard on you."

"It was hard on all of us. Mikey was a senior in high school himself, but Ian and Slade put their own college plans on hold to come home to help keep the family together. Truly, I owe them a lot. Which is why I pretty much got used to them sticking their nose into my personal business." She tried to lighten the sudden seriousness of the conversation. "Can you believe they went so far as to read my diary? Nothing was sacred. Absolutely nothing."

Caleb's lips twitched. "Will you let me read it?"

"No." She glowered at him. "Don't even think about it."

"Raine!" her brother bellowed from the bathroom.

She ground her teeth together, tempted once again to tell Michael to go find a hotel. "Now what's the problem?" she asked.

"My problem?" Her brother stomped out of her bathroom, a deep scowl creasing his forehead, and it took her a moment to realize he had her pregnancy test kit clutched in his hand. "Here's my problem. Are you pregnant?"

CHAPTER THIRTEEN

RAINE'S eyes widened in horror as her brother, the human bulldozer, revealed her most painful, shameful secret. She glanced frantically at Caleb in time to watch all the color drain from his face as he stared with utter disbelief at the pregnancy test kit.

And in that one awful, terrible moment she knew. No matter what he'd said earlier, he didn't trust her. Would likely never trust her.

Which meant he'd never love her the way she loved him.

There was a moment of dead silence before she moved, snatching the kit out of her brother's hand, wishing she dared to smack him with it. "No, I'm not pregnant." The stomach cramps she'd experienced earlier that morning convinced her that her period wasn't far off. "Keep your nose out of my business."

"Raine, you having a baby is my business. Our business. The child would be our niece or nephew. Of course, we'd help you raise the baby if some jerk took off and abandoned you." Michael glared at Caleb.

Caleb opened his mouth to speak and she sent him a

dark look, warning him not to say a word, either in his own defense about the child not being his or about the assault. "Leave Caleb alone, Mikey. I mean it. You're my brother and I love you, but that does not give you the right to intrude into my personal life."

Her brother raised his hands innocently, as if realizing he might have pushed too far. "Hey, I'm just saying-we'll stand by you."

She let out a sigh, knowing that at least that much was right. Her brother had always been there for her. And if she had gotten pregnant, her brothers would support her.

Unlike Caleb, whose face was suddenly completely devoid of all expression.

Obviously, she and Caleb needed to talk. Yet at the same time she couldn't help feeling irritated at his reaction. Why did she always have to explain herself? Couldn't he ever just once give her the benefit of doubt? What good would any explanation be if he refused to believe in her?

She'd known earlier that Caleb's lack of trust wasn't something she could help him overcome.

This was only irrefutable proof that he'd need to fix his problems on his own.

An awkward silence fell and she dreaded the conversation she and Caleb needed to have. "Mikey, give us a few minutes alone, would you?" she asked softly.

"Uh, yeah. Sure." Michael glanced between the two of them, with a shrug. "Actually, I was looking for a razor so I could shave." He scrubbed a hand over his jaw. "Can I borrow one of yours?"

"Help yourself," she said, knowing he would anyway.

After her brother left them alone, she turned to Caleb. "I'm sorry. I tried to tell you my brothers were over-protective."

"You thought you were pregnant?" His tone was accusing.

She lifted her chin. "I guess attempting a second chance wasn't a good idea after all."

A flash of disbelief glittered in his eyes. "What sort of second chance did we have if you weren't honest with me? You never said a word about possibly being pregnant."

She stared at him, wondering if he was using this as an excuse to quit on the relationship before it even started. "I told you about the sexual assault. Didn't it occur to you that pregnancy might be a consequence? Besides, what difference does it make now? I used the test, I'm not pregnant."

He blew out a breath and turned away, avoiding her gaze. "Why didn't you say anything to me about it? You told me everything else, didn't you?"

She shook her head, tears stinging her eyes. This was his issue, not hers. "And if I say yes, I've told you everything else, will you believe me?"

When he didn't immediately answer, she swallowed hard. "I'm sorry, Caleb, but this isn't going to work." Trying to ignore the way her heart was aching, she walked over to her apartment door and opened it. "Thanks for driving me home. I'm sure I'll see you around at work."

Caleb stared at her for a long moment, and then walked past her. "Yeah. See you around," he muttered as he left the apartment.

Fighting tears, she slowly closed the apartment door

behind him and then leaned heavily against it. Her stomach clenched and the familiar nausea that she now knew was a result of stress returned with a vengeance.

Caleb hadn't believed in her before the assault and he clearly didn't now. Even after the closeness they'd shared.

This time she knew their relationship was over.

Caleb left Raine's apartment and walked outside, reeling from their argument.

He couldn't believe she'd never told him her fears about being pregnant as a result of the assault. Of course he'd considered the possibility but hadn't pushed for the details. When she hadn't mentioned it, he'd assumed it wasn't a problem.

What else hadn't she told him?

Earlier that morning, he'd been angry when he'd thought she'd taken off without a word. He could readily admit that he'd overreacted, automatically thinking the worst.

When he'd found her outside, sitting on the deck with Grizzly, he'd felt like a fool. Especially when she'd given him a look full of reproach. He'd known then he needed to stop reading the worst into everything she said or did.

But this was different. They'd grown closer together over these past few days. They'd spent the night making love. Why would she keep secrets from him at this point in their relationship?

It was clear that if her brother hadn't found the test kit and bluntly confronted her with it, she wouldn't have mentioned the possibility at all.

He was so lost in thought he didn't realize he'd walked several blocks past his car until he came upon a stop sign for a major road. Muttering a curse, he spun on his heel and stalked back to where he'd left his car.

As he opened the door, about to slide in, he couldn't help glancing up at Raine's apartment window. Of course she wasn't standing there, watching him. He climbed in behind the wheel and slammed the door behind him.

He hoped, for her sake, she did tell her brother what had happened. Raine had been through a terrible ordeal. She needed all the support she could get.

His cellphone rang, interrupting his thoughts. He glanced at the number, surprised to realize it was the hospital. His dad? His heart rate spiked in alarm as he quickly answered. "Hello?"

"Caleb? Can you pick me up?" After yesterday's visit, his father sounded surprisingly upbeat. "Doc says I'm ready to be discharged."

"Really? Sure, of course I'll pick you up. I can be there in a few minutes."

"Are you bringing Raine with you?"

His father's innocent question sent a shaft of pain through his heart. Raine would have loved to come with him to pick up his father. For a moment the reality of what had just happened upstairs in her apartment hit hard.

Their relationship was over. For good.

But this wasn't the time to tell his father the news. Not yet. "No, her brother is in town right now, visiting with her." He tried not to let his father hear the desolation in his tone. "But I'll let her know you're coming home. She'll be thrilled."

"Okay." His father readily accepted the excuse. "And don't forget we have to pick up Grizz on the way home."

"I won't forget. See you soon, Dad."

Caleb started the car and headed straight over to the hospital, grateful for something else to think about rather than the mess he'd made of his personal life.

Because there was no denying how lonely his house would feel now that both Raine and Grizzly were gone.

Caleb had been fully prepared to stay with his father during the first week after his hospitalization to help care for him at home. But surprisingly his father seemed to have taken Raine's advice to heart.

"Caleb, this is Marlene Fitzgerald, one of the volunteers at the animal shelter," his father said, introducing him to a spry, silver-haired woman standing next to him. She looked to be similar in age to his father, which by itself was unusual, since his father's women in the past had all been much younger. "Marlene, this is my son, Caleb. He's a doctor on staff here in the emergency department at Trinity Medical Center. He chose the path of taking care of people rather than animals."

Caleb stepped forward to take the older woman's hand. "Hi, Marlene. It's nice to meet you."

"Same here, Caleb." Marlene smiled, blushing a bit. "I hope you don't mind if I temporarily move in to help care for your father for a few days."

Temporarily move in? He arched a brow at his father. "Uh, no. Of course not. But I can help too, Dad. You've had major surgery, and I've arranged to take some time off work."

"There's no need for you to take off work for me," his father said gruffly. "I appreciate your efforts, but Marlene offered to help and I think together we'll be able to manage just fine."

"If you're sure…" Caleb gave in, as it appeared his father had planned everything out. "I'd still like to stop by each day to see how things are going."

"I'll take you up on that offer. Can't pass up the opportunity to get a house call," his father joked.

Caleb carried his father's belongings as Marlene pushed his wheelchair down to the hospital lobby. He went round to bring up the car and, as promised, stopped by his house on the way home to pick up Grizzly.

Marlene didn't seem to mind the dog, greeting Grizz with enthusiasm. She clearly loved animals as much as his father did.

He wanted to believe Marlene and his father were meant to be together, but the old suspicions wouldn't go away. Marlene seemed perfect now, but his father's relationships never seemed to last.

After dropping Marlene and his father off at home, taking time to ensure his dad was settled comfortably in his favorite recliner, with Grizz at his feet, Caleb headed home.

Greeted by nothing more than the echo of his own voice, he called the hospital to notify them he was available to work if needed after all. They promised to call if something opened up or if someone called in sick. Dejected, he stared out at his back yard, wondering what to do with the extra time on his hands.

If Raine was here, he would have been thrilled to

have more time off work. But now he would rather have something to do to keep his mind off her.

Raine had been right about one thing. His trust issues were his own problem to fix. Keeping secrets wasn't the way to inspire trust, yet even before that he'd known he'd made mistakes.

Mistakes he wasn't sure how to fix.

Was he doomed to the same fate as his father? To have nothing but one failed relationship after another?

As much as he didn't want to go down that same path, he was at a loss as to how to break the pattern.

Raine sank down onto her sofa, overwhelmingly relieved when Mikey finally took off to attend his training session. She wanted, needed time alone to pull her battered emotions together.

She couldn't help replaying that moment her brother had asked if she was pregnant over and over in her mind. Her stomach clenched painfully. Even though she knew that Caleb hadn't fully trusted her before then, the shattered expression in his eyes still haunted her.

Did Caleb have a right to be upset? Should she have told him her fears?

Maybe.

She and Caleb had been doomed, right from the beginning. She'd been right to break things off before the assault.

The past would always stand between them.

Spice jumped up on the sofa beside her and she drew the cat into her arms, cuddling her soft fur. If only people were more like animals, full of unconditional love.

Her brothers loved her unconditionally. Was it unfair to expect the same from Caleb?

She didn't think so. Her parents had died too young, but she'd always known how much they'd loved and cared for each other. She wanted and deserved the same sort of love.

Since sitting around and wallowing in self-pity wasn't an option, she decided to spend the rest of her afternoon at the animal shelter. With Dr. Frank gone, they were probably short-handed. And she'd rather be busy to keep her mind off of Caleb.

She took a quick shower, shocked to discover her instincts were right. She'd gotten her period.

She'd begun blowdrying her hair when her phone rang. For one heart-stopping moment she wondered if the caller was Caleb. Was he calling to apologize and beg her to come back?

And why was she even tempted by the possibility when nothing had changed?

She dashed over to the phone, slowing down with a sharp stab of disappointment when the number displayed an unknown caller on her caller ID.

Letting the call go to her answering-machine, she headed back towards the bathroom to finish up. But stopped dead in her tracks when a familiar voice came over the speaker.

"Raine, this is Detective Carol Blanchard with the Milwaukee Police Department. Please call me as soon as you get this message. We need your help in identifying a suspect we have in custody. We believe he could possibly be the man who raped you."

They had a suspect? Raine dropped the brush she was holding, unable to believe it. Her fingers trembled so badly she had difficulty dialing Detective Blanchard's phone number. She told herself not to get her hopes up too high, but she held her breath, waiting for the detective to answer.

"Detective Blanchard."

"Detective, this is Raine Hart returning your phone call."

"Raine, I'm so glad you called me back so quickly. I know you don't remember the man who assaulted you, but we wanted to have you come down to the station to look at a line-up anyway. Our hope is that you can maybe pick out the guy who was at the nightclub the night of your assault."

"A line-up?" Her mouth went desert dry and her heart thudded painfully in her chest. "Uh, sure. If you think it might help."

"We do think this would help," Detective Blanchard assured her. "The DNA testing is going to take time, and we'd like to at least place this suspect at the scene of the crime. Could you be here in an hour?"

An hour? So soon? She swallowed a momentary flash of panic. "Of course. No problem."

"Great, we'll see you in an hour, then."

Raine hung up the phone, feeling jittery. She hurried to finish in the bathroom, wishing more than anything that Caleb was here with her. If they hadn't argued, he would have gone with her for moral support.

She pushed away the useless thoughts. But as she used the hairdryer, she couldn't help worrying.

What if she couldn't pick this guy out as one of the men who were at the After Dark nightclub that night? And if she couldn't identify him, would he go free?

CHAPTER FOURTEEN

As Raine walked up the concrete steps leading into the police station she saw a familiar figure walking down the stairs in the opposite direction. The woman walked with her shoulders hunched and her head down to avoid direct eye contact with anyone.

But Raine still recognized her. Helen Shore. Her sexual assault patient from the ED.

The knot in her stomach tightened. Had Helen successfully picked the suspect out of the line-up? Or was the fate of this man going to rest solely on her shoulders?

Her footsteps slowed as a tidal wave of doubt swept in. What if she picked the wrong man? Or, worse, what if she picked the suspect they had, but he was actually innocent?

The DNA evidence would eventually exonerate him if that were the case, but not for several weeks yet.

She took a deep breath, and walked into the police station. Detective Blanchard was waiting for her.

"Hi, Raine. How are you doing?" The detective's expression radiated true concern.

The tenseness in her stomach eased a bit. "Pretty good, all things considered."

Detective Blanchard's gaze was sharply assessing. "You look good," she said slowly. "Like you've really recovered. I'm glad. Well, are you ready?"

No, she wasn't ready. But she nodded. "Yes, but what happens if I can't pick this guy out of the line-up? Does he walk away?"

"Come with me, and I'll explain how this works." The detective led the way into a small room, with a one-way mirror lining the wall. "This suspect isn't going to walk away, no matter what happens here today. I don't want you to feel pressure to make the so-called right identification. We have enough evidence to hold this guy for a while. So don't worry about him being back on the street, because that's not going to happen. Just relax and do your best."

"Okay." She placed a hand over her heart, willing her pulse to slow down, and swallowed hard. "I'm ready."

Detective Blanchard hit a button on the intercom. "We're ready—bring the suspects in."

Raine watched as six men walked into the brightly lit anteroom in single file, each going to their assigned numbers. They all stood staring straight ahead, their hands down at their sides. A tingle of apprehension slithered down her spine, even though she knew they couldn't see her. She clasped her arms over her chest, wishing more than anything that Caleb was here to hold her.

She took her time, looking at each of the men. When she reached suspect number five, the tingle turned into a full-fledged shiver.

He was the silent one who'd been there that night. She was sure of it. But, still, she forced herself to look at suspect number six, too. And then Detective Blanchard gave the order for the men to turn to the right and then to the left, so she could get a thorough look at their profiles.

Her gaze went back to suspect number five. She was absolutely certain he was one of the two guys who'd been next to her that night. She remembered the way he'd watched her so intently without saying much, letting his buddy do all the talking for him.

"Number five," she said, looking at Detective Blanchard. "I recognize suspect number five as being in the nightclub that night. He and another man bought me a drink, and I don't remember anything after that."

"Are you sure?" Detective Blanchard asked, her gaze impassive.

For a moment her heart sank. Had she picked the wrong man? She turned back and looked at them again, but she knew number five was the man who'd been there. "Yes, I'm sure." Her voice rang out with confidence. "Number five."

A smile broke out on Detective Blanchard's face. She reached over to touch the intercom button. "Thanks, we're finished here." The men filed out of the room.

The detective turned toward her. "Good job, Raine. Number five is the suspect we arrested. His name is Colin Ward and your positive ID will help us when we present our case to the grand jury."

Overwhelming relief washed over her. Colin Ward? Sounded like such an average name. "What happened?" she asked curiously. "How did you end up arresting him?"

"We set up a sting operation at the After Dark nightclub with one of our young, very attractive female officers. We also had a cop working undercover behind the bar and we caught him spiking her drink with Rohypnol. The bartender quickly swapped it out but she played along, as if she was drunk. Colin Ward insisted on helping her out to her car, and once he'd stashed her in the passenger seat and slid behind the wheel with her keys, we nailed him."

"I can't believe he did it again," she whispered.

"He's a predator, no question about it. And when the DNA match is confirmed, and we're very sure it will be, this guy will go to jail for a long time."

She was glad, fiercely glad, that he'd been caught. How many others had he raped? She knew only too often that many women didn't come forward after something like that. Especially when they couldn't remember what had really happened.

She wanted to ask if Helen Shore had been able to identify him, too, but she held back, unwilling to break her patient's confidentiality. Helen's ability to ID him wouldn't matter as she herself had been able to pick him out without a problem.

Detective Blanchard walked her back outside, telling her she'd be in touch when and if the case went to trial. The detective thought that if the DNA evidence was positive, Colin Ward would cop a plea.

Raine nodded, hardly listening. No matter what happened from here, her nightmare was over. She'd thought she'd feel better once the guy was caught, and she did, except there was a part of her that still felt empty.

Because she didn't have Caleb.

She walked to her car and slid behind the wheel. She was tempted, very tempted, to call Caleb. He was the only one who'd understand how she felt. And in spite of their most recent break-up, she knew he'd want to know. She went so far as to pull out her cellphone, bringing up his number, but then hesitated.

No. She flipped her phone closed. She needed to figure out how to move forward with her life without him. Because even if she called him now, and they managed to mend their rift from this morning, how long would the peace last?

Only until the next time she did something stupid. Or until the next time she grew tired of his inability to trust her.

She loved him, but they didn't have a chance at a future. Better to figure out a way to get over him, once and for all.

Caleb's father called two days after he'd been discharged, asking if Caleb could come over for a while because Marlene had to go and help her daughter, who needed an urgent babysitter for her sick child. He readily agreed, heading over right away.

Grizzly met him at the door, waving his tail excitedly. "Hi, Grizz, how are you? Taking good care of Dad, hmm?"

"Caleb? Is that you?" his father called from the kitchen.

"Yes, I'm here." Caleb made his way through the house into the kitchen. "Has Marlene left already?" he asked.

"Yeah, her daughter had to be at work by nine, so she went over first thing."

"I hope she doesn't bring germs back to you," Caleb said, pulling up a chair and sitting down beside his dad. "You need to stay as healthy as possible."

"Marlene said the same thing. She's just as worried as you are. I'm sure I'll be fine," his father said. "I'm surprised you didn't bring Raine with you. How is she?"

Caleb had dodged questions about Raine in the past few days, but he couldn't keep lying to his dad. He blew out a heavy breath. "She's fine, as far as I know. But we're not seeing each other any more."

"What?" His father glared at him. "Why not? What happened? Raine was perfect for you, Caleb. A keeper!"

He couldn't suppress a flash of annoyance. "And how would you know a keeper, Dad? You're hardly the expert. None of the women you picked stuck around long enough to be a keeper. What's the longest relationship you had since Mom left? Three years?"

His father's eyes widened and his frankly wounded expression hit Caleb like a punch to the gut.

His breath hissed out between his teeth. What was wrong with him? This wasn't his father's fault. "I'm sorry. I shouldn't have said that."

His father stared at him for a moment. "No, don't apologize. I never realized you felt that way."

Caleb winced. "I should have just kept my mouth shut," he muttered.

"No, I think you need to understand, Caleb. The reason I had trouble holding relationships together after your mother left was largely my own fault."

Caleb couldn't help but agree to a certain extent, because his father had obviously picked some losers.

"No, it wasn't your fault, Dad. The women you were with made lousy choices."

"Listen, Caleb. I didn't love them. I couldn't love them, because I was still in love with your mother."

Caleb stared at his father in shock. "You loved her? Even after she left us?"

His father's smile was sad. "Son, you don't always control who you love. Your mother got pregnant with you and we tried to make a marriage work. But she was young and a very talented dancer. She talked constantly about pursuing a dancing career. When she told me she was moving to New York, alone, I wasn't entirely surprised."

He'd heard the story of his mother getting a part in the Broadway play so the fact that she'd left them to dance wasn't a surprise. But his father's easy acceptance of her leaving was. "She left us both for her own selfish reasons and that's okay?"

"She was young," his father defended. "And I knew she wasn't ready to settle down. But I loved her. Even after she left, I didn't stop loving her."

"So why the string of women?" he asked.

His father flushed. "I felt bad for you, Caleb. I wanted you to have a mother. And I can't deny I was looking for some companionship, too."

Caleb scrubbed a hand over his face. "I understand. I can't blame you."

"You're missing the point. I couldn't give the women in my life the love they deserved. And they obviously knew that. So that's why those relationships ended. Carmen put up with me the longest, until she realized I wouldn't return her love. I think there was a part of me that kept holding back, hoping your mother would return once she'd gotten her dancing out of her system."

Caleb frowned. "She's married to someone else now. Heck, she has a new family of her own." He couldn't quite hide his bitterness. He'd reached out to his mother once, after high school, but she hadn't been very interested in the family she'd left behind.

"I know." His father didn't look surprised. "But it still took my heart a long time to give up hope. But don't blame the women who've come and gone over the years, Caleb. The blame is mine."

Caleb sat there, dumbfounded by the turn in the conversation. He sensed his father was telling the truth. For so long he had blamed the women in his father's life for not being trustworthy. And he'd blamed his father for his poor choices.

But it had never occurred to him how his father had ended up sabotaging his own relationships because he'd still loved his son's mother.

Had he let his own bitterness after the incident with Tabitha do the same? Ruin his chance at a decent relationship?

"If you love Raine with your whole heart and soul, you need to fight for her," his father urged in a low voice. "Don't let her go, Caleb."

Was it really that easy? He loved Raine. With his whole heart and soul. And he knew, honestly knew, she wouldn't intentionally hurt him.

His dad was right. Raine was a keeper.

He jumped to his feet. "Dad, I have to go." Then he realized he couldn't leave and abruptly sat back down.

"Sorry, I almost forgot. I can't go right now. I'll wait for Marlene to come back."

"Tell you what. Throw something together for me to eat for lunch, and then you can go." His father idly rubbed his chest. "I promise I'll do my physical therapy exercises."

"Really?" Caleb glanced at his father doubtfully, desire warring with duty. "Are you sure?"

"I'm sure." His father put a hand on Grizzly's head. "Grizz and I will be just fine. I'll call you if I need something."

"Okay." Caleb grinned, clapping his dad on the back. "Thanks. For everything."

He was going to win Raine back, although he knew it wouldn't be an easy task.

He needed help. And he wasn't afraid to use every possible resource at his disposal.

Raine glanced up in surprise when her doorbell buzzer went off. Mikey? If so, her brother was early.

"Yes?"

"Raine? It's Caleb. I'd like to talk to you if you have a minute."

Caleb? Her heart squeezed in her chest and hope, ever foolish, surged. "Uh, sure. Come on up."

"Actually, I need you to come down."

She frowned. Why did she need to come down?

Admittedly curious, she grabbed her keys and headed out of the apartment, taking the stairs down to the lobby level. When she went outside, she was surprised to see Caleb standing there with Rusty, the sweet Irish setter from the animal shelter.

"Rusty!" she exclaimed, going down into a crouch to greet the dog. He waved his tail excitedly, lavishing her with doggie kisses that she laughingly avoided as much as possible. "It's so good to see him. I'm surprised he's letting you near him without growling," she said. "He's normally afraid of men."

"I know. It took me a few days to win him over, but I did. He's not afraid of me. I'm taking that as a sign we were meant to be together."

"You adopted him?" She was glad Rusty was going to a good home, but she couldn't hide the wistfulness in her tone.

"I'd like to. But that depends on you."

She frowned, slowly rising to her feet. "What do you mean?"

"Rusty has learned to trust me, and I'm hoping you will, too, when I ask for you to give me another chance."

Hope lunged in her heart, but she held back. "I don't know if that's a good idea," she began.

"Wait, please hear me out," he interrupted. "You were right, my problems weren't about you. They were about me. I needed to learn to trust myself. To let myself love you. It's a long story, but my dad made me realize what an idiot I've been."

His dad? The kernel of hope grew bigger.

"I love you, Raine. More than I can say. Every time I pushed you away, it was because I was holding back, protecting myself from being hurt. But I've been hurting since I walked away from you. And even if you send me away right now, I'm still going to love you."

She wanted to believe him, she really did. "I love you,

too, Caleb. But sometimes love isn't enough. I don't think I can live with a man who constantly doubts me."

Contrary to her words, his face brightened. "But that's just it. I trust both of us. All I'm asking right now is for a chance to prove it to you."

Rusty nudged her hand, asking for attention. "You're not fighting fair," she murmured, glancing between the dog and the man she loved, who managed to gang up on her.

"I'm fighting for my life, Raine," he said, taking her comment seriously. "But I understand I've hurt you, even though I didn't mean to. So if you need time, that's fine, you can take all the time you need. But know that no matter what happens, I'll be waiting for you."

His willingness to back off surprised her. And she realized she couldn't let him take all the blame. "Not everything was your fault, Caleb. I didn't always confide in you. Living with three older brothers taught me that I couldn't talk about everything that bothered me because they would make such a big deal out of every little thing. So I learned to suppress a lot of what I was thinking and feeling. I'm sure my tendency to hide my deepest feelings didn't help your ability to trust me."

"Sweet of you to try to take the blame, Raine, but it's not your fault by a long shot. But if you're willing to give me a second chance, I won't argue."

Wasn't this the third chance? Maybe, but who was counting? Not her. Not any more. She was lucky enough to have people in her life who loved her unconditionally. Wasn't it time she did the same? Didn't Caleb deserve her unconditional love?

"I am willing," she said softly.

"You are?" He looked afraid to hope.

"Yes. Because I love you, too. I've been miserable without you. If you really think we can make this work, I'm more than willing to try again."

"Thank God," he murmured, reaching over to pull her into a warm embrace. "Things will be different this time, Raine. You'll see."

"I know." She lifted her eyes to his and he bent to capture her mouth in a searing kiss. Instantly she melted against him, longing for more.

"Wanna come to my place?" Caleb asked huskily, when she finally came up for air. "You could help Rusty get acquainted in his new home."

"Sure, I'll come over for a bit. But don't worry, he's going to love his new home," she assured him, giving the dog's silky ears a good rub.

"I don't want to rush you, Raine," Caleb said in a low voice. "But my home can be your home too. Rusty and I will be waiting for you whenever you're ready."

She went still. "Really? Just like that?"

He nodded, no sign of hesitation. "Just like that."

Wow. She wasn't sure what to say. "I should probably tell you that the police caught the guy who assaulted me."

"They did?" Caleb looked surprised. "That's good news, Raine. I'm happy for you."

"I had to pick him out of a line-up," she confessed. "I wanted you with me so badly, but it all worked out. He's going to stay in jail without bail until the DNA results are in."

"I'm sorry I wasn't there for you," Caleb said, pulling

her close for another hug. "I hope one day you'll be able to put all this behind you."

"I will," she said confidently. She couldn't help wondering if her relationship with Caleb hadn't somehow grown stronger through everything that had happened. If she hadn't changed, would the two of them be standing there right now? She doubted it. "I can face anything with you beside me."

Caleb gave her another one-armed hug, the other hand firmly on Rusty's leash. "I feel the same way, Raine. As if I can conquer anything with you at my side. I love you so much."

"I love you, too." Her smile shimmered straight from her heart as she tugged Rusty's leash from his hand. "Take us home, Caleb."

His eyes lit up with hope and promise. "Yes. Let's go home."

SEPTEMBER 2010 HARDBACK TITLES

ROMANCE

A Stormy Greek Marriage	Lynne Graham
Unworldly Secretary, Untamed Greek	Kim Lawrence
The Sabbides Secret Baby	Jacqueline Baird
The Undoing of de Luca	Kate Hewitt
Katrakis's Last Mistress	Caitlin Crews
Surrender to Her Spanish Husband	Maggie Cox
Passion, Purity and the Prince	Annie West
For Revenge or Redemption?	Elizabeth Power
Red Wine and Her Sexy Ex	Kate Hardy
Every Girl's Secret Fantasy	Robyn Grady
Cattle Baron Needs a Bride	Margaret Way
Passionate Chef, Ice Queen Boss	Jennie Adams
Sparks Fly with Mr Mayor	Teresa Carpenter
Rescued in a Wedding Dress	Cara Colter
Wedding Date with the Best Man	Melissa McClone
Maid for the Single Dad	Susan Meier
Alessandro and the Cheery Nanny	Amy Andrews
Valentino's Pregnancy Bombshell	Amy Andrews

HISTORICAL

Reawakening Miss Calverley	Sylvia Andrew
The Unmasking of a Lady	Emily May
Captured by the Warrior	Meriel Fuller

MEDICAL™

Dating the Millionaire Doctor	Marion Lennox
A Knight for Nurse Hart	Laura Iding
A Nurse to Tame the Playboy	Maggie Kingsley
Village Midwife, Blushing Bride	Gill Sanderson

0810 Gen Std LP

MILLS & BOON

SEPTEMBER 2010 LARGE PRINT TITLES

ROMANCE

Virgin on Her Wedding Night	Lynne Graham
Blackwolf's Redemption	Sandra Marton
The Shy Bride	Lucy Monroe
Penniless and Purchased	Julia James
Beauty and the Reclusive Prince	Raye Morgan
Executive: Expecting Tiny Twins	Barbara Hannay
A Wedding at Leopard Tree Lodge	Liz Fielding
Three Times A Bridesmaid...	Nicola Marsh

HISTORICAL

The Viscount's Unconventional Bride	Mary Nichols
Compromising Miss Milton	Michelle Styles
Forbidden Lady	Anne Herries

MEDICAL™

The Doctor's Lost-and-Found Bride	Kate Hardy
Miracle: Marriage Reunited	Anne Fraser
A Mother for Matilda	Amy Andrews
The Boss and Nurse Albright	Lynne Marshall
New Surgeon at Ashvale A&E	Joanna Neil
Desert King, Doctor Daddy	Meredith Webber

™ MILLS & BOON®

OCTOBER 2010 HARDBACK TITLES

ROMANCE

The Reluctant Surrender	Penny Jordan
Shameful Secret, Shotgun Wedding	Sharon Kendrick
The Virgin's Choice	Jennie Lucas
Scandal: Unclaimed Love-Child	Melanie Milburne
Powerful Greek, Housekeeper Wife	Robyn Donald
Hired by Her Husband	Anne McAllister
Snowbound Seduction	Helen Brooks
A Mistake, A Prince and A Pregnancy	Maisey Yates
Champagne with a Celebrity	Kate Hardy
When He was Bad...	Anne Oliver
Accidentally Pregnant!	Rebecca Winters
Star-Crossed Sweethearts	Jackie Braun
A Miracle for His Secret Son	Barbara Hannay
Proud Rancher, Precious Bundle	Donna Alward
Cowgirl Makes Three	Myrna Mackenzie
Secret Prince, Instant Daddy!	Raye Morgan
Officer, Surgeon...Gentleman!	Janice Lynn
Midwife in the Family Way	Fiona McArthur

HISTORICAL

Innocent Courtesan to Adventurer's Bride	Louise Allen
Disgrace and Desire	Sarah Mallory
The Viking's Captive Princess	Michelle Styles

MEDICAL™

Bachelor of the Baby Ward	Meredith Webber
Fairytale on the Children's Ward	Meredith Webber
Playboy Under the Mistletoe	Joanna Neil
Their Marriage Miracle	Sue MacKay

0910 Gen Std LP

MILLS & BOON

OCTOBER 2010 LARGE PRINT TITLES

ROMANCE

Marriage: To Claim His Twins	Penny Jordan
The Royal Baby Revelation	Sharon Kendrick
Under the Spaniard's Lock and Key	Kim Lawrence
Sweet Surrender with the Millionaire	Helen Brooks
Miracle for the Girl Next Door	Rebecca Winters
Mother of the Bride	Caroline Anderson
What's A Housekeeper To Do?	Jennie Adams
Tipping the Waitress with Diamonds	Nina Harrington

HISTORICAL

Practical Widow to Passionate Mistress	Louise Allen
Major Westhaven's Unwilling Ward	Emily Bascom
Her Banished Lord	Carol Townend

MEDICAL™

The Nurse's Brooding Boss	Laura Iding
Emergency Doctor and Cinderella	Melanie Milburne
City Surgeon, Small Town Miracle	Marion Lennox
Bachelor Dad, Girl Next Door	Sharon Archer
A Baby for the Flying Doctor	Lucy Clark
Nurse, Nanny...Bride!	Alison Roberts